30 DAYS

K. LARSEN

This Novel is a work of fiction. All of the characters, organizations and events portrayed herein are either products of the author's imagination, or used fictitiously.

BOOKS BY K. LARSEN

Jezebel

Lying In Wait

The Brother

The Tutor

Imposter

Missed Connection

The Marriage Pact

Killing The Sun

Unbound Pages

30 Days

Committed

Dating Delaney

Saving Caroline

-BLOODLINES SERIES-

Tug of War

Objective

Resistance

Target 84

ACKNOWLEDGMENTS

First and foremost, I would like to thank my sister and all my parents for their encouragement and support.

My sister is my rock, and I dedicate this book to her. I also thank my wonderful daughter: Bella, for always making me smile.

Thank you to my husband and friends for everything-giving me stuff to write about and being excited for me and especially for not laughing in my face when I said I was writing a book! To Chrissy Anderson for writing THE LIFE LIST and inspiring me to grab hold of this life and fight for love and happiness without shame.

You're awesome Chrissy!

PROLOGUE

THE LIST! I can't forget the list. I rip it from the wall fold it up and stuff it in my sports bra. My heart is beating wildly in my chest. I feel frantic and I'm starting to sweat. I pull on my hoodie sans hood strings of course, slip my feet into my lace-less Keds, and make my way to Manny's sleeping form.

It's eerily quiet in the corridor right now. Just the faint hum of the ice machine and various beeps and buzzes from patients' rooms. I quietly sneak around the nurses' station desk and crouch down to Manny. I'm so sorry. I really do like you. Please forgive me. I tug his wallet out of his back pocket and remove all the cash. A hundred dollars will be plenty to tide me over until the morning. I stuff the cash in my sports bra. I unclip Manny's employee badge from the front of his shirt, toss the wallet on the desk next to his head, and quickly walk down the hall.

Every noise, every beep, every voice makes me panic and stop moving. I press myself into the wall until I'm sure it's nothing. This is crazy, Elle. What are you doing? I silently scold myself. When I'm sure the coast is clear I walk to the main doors of our floor and hold Manny's badge up to the magnetic reader. A slight click alerts me that all I have to do is push the door in front of me and I'm as good as free. My hand shakes as I raise it up to the door. It feels heavy and like someone else's arm. With my palm on the door I lean into my arm slightly until it opens just enough for me to slip through.

I try to walk as inconspicuously as possible to the elevators and punch the Down button. There is no one in the hallway except a few passing laundry aides who pay me no mind. The fact that I'm wearing scrubs, a hoodie, and white sneakers is probably my only saving grace. I blend in pretty well. The elevator dings and the doors open. I put one foot in front of the other until I'm safely inside before hitting the Lobby button. My skin feels like it's on fire. My breath is quick and shallow and my heart is beating so fiercely in my rib cage that I'm afraid it might crack bone.

The elevator dings again and the doors slide open. I step out of the metal box, turn left, and, keeping my chin down, head for the glass front doors. The fifty-foot walk seems to take forever. There is a woman sitting behind the information desk who's watching me. I tilt my head up and smile at her. She smiles back. The revolving doors close around me as I step into their spin and then I'm out.

It's the end of July or the first week of August. I'm not sure which. It's muggy and damp and hot out. The humidity assaults my lungs when I try to inhale. It's definitely too hot for a sweatshirt but I only have a sports bra on underneath it. I keep walking further and further away from the hospital until I'm sure that if someone looked out a window they wouldn't see me. I walk into the nearest convenience store to buy a pack of gum and a bottle of water. The air conditioning in the store feels heavenly. I'm dripping with sweat from my walk here and nerves.

I did it. I'm out! A wave of relief washes over me, leaving

me temporarily giddy. When I exit the store I notice a few taxis parked and waiting across the street. I make my way over to one of them. "Could you take me to a cheap hotel?" I ask the cabby through the open window.

"How cheap?"

"Dirt cheap," I reply. He nods his head at me and I open the back door and climb in. He drives four blocks before pulling up in front of a dilapidated brick building. "They rent by the hour," he informs me.

I didn't mean this cheap but honestly it will do. I hand him a ten-dollar bill and get out of the cab. When I finally check in, paying for one night, I'm left with fifty-two dollars and change. The cab ride to my house from here will be at least thirty dollars. I lie down on top of the blankets fully clothed and stare at the chipping ceiling paint. Jenny, we did it. I'm out. Almost free. Stay with me. The bed is lumpy and the room smells funny. I close my eyes, trying to ignore my surroundings, and an hour later I fall asleep.

I wake with a start. I'm groggy and can't remember where I am. It's disorienting. When my brain catches up with me I let out a squeal of joy. This is the dirty, cheap hotel. I am not in my sterile room. I escaped.

PRESENT

ELLE

DAY 1

The sun is shining through the sheer curtains. I stretch my arms and legs, arching my back. I haven't slept so well in a long time. I feel rested. When I open my eyes the sheer blue of the bedroom walls calms me. I can hear the waves lapping the sand outside and seagulls squawking. It's going to be a good day, I can feel it. I smile as I roll out of bed and start the coffee maker before brushing my teeth. Back in the kitchen I grab the new mug I bought yesterday that reads "step aside coffee, this is a job for alcohol." It made me giggle, so I bought it. Setting it on the counter, I turn and reach for the fridge handle. The list hangs directly in my line of sight. "Have dinner alone" is at the top of it.

I yank the door open, grab the creamer, and head outside with my coffee and a cinnamon roll from the bakery up the street. *Morning, Jenny. This is day one, Sister! I'm going to tackle that stupid list if it's the last thing I do. Love you.* I sink my teeth into the cinnamon roll and moan. Inspecting it further, it has got to be the best cinnamon roll I've ever put in my mouth. Its perfect parts icing, dough, and cinnamon, and I think I could eat ten of them. I try to savor it, really, I do, but I pretty much shoved as much as possible in my mouth and finish it in three bites. I pick up the complimentary paper left on the patio set every morning and thumb through the pages leisurely as I finish my coffee.

I choke on a sip of my coffee when I see my picture, the same one from the TV, printed on the back page of the third section. It's a missing persons' type ad but also goes on to say that I am a possible danger to myself and to please call Mick Tyson with information. Who is Mick Tyson? I grab my Kindle and open up the web to search him. I really wish I had my laptop.

"Mick has a 90% success rate when searching for missing persons.

Supply him with the information on the 'Locate Missing Person' sheet and he will do the rest. Everything is confidential.

For a free confidential & discreet consultation, call 888-800-3455."

I blow out a breath. Great. Not entirely the perfect morning I had planned. Well, Mick, I hate to foil your plans, but Elle Darling is not going to be found. I have thirty things to get done and intend on doing them. It helps that I'm paying for everything in cash. I'm not as stupid as Ryan thinks. With newfound determination I decide to take a shopping trip today and give myself a makeover.

I hit the salon first, indulging in a long overdue manicure and a pedicure. While my nails are drying, I get an amazing facial that leaves me feeling like a new person. Lastly, I get a haircut. I've always kept my hair long, at least halfway down my back, but I have the stylist cut in some long wispy bangs and bring it up so my newly brunette hair skims my shoulders. I look better than I have in months. Healthy. Alive. Almost vibrant. I leave the salon with a smile on my face and a spring in my step. I feel wonderful and I haven't felt that way in years.

Now it's time for some serious shopping. I want a new look for my wardrobe. I've always dressed fairly preppy but I think it's time to go with a more laid-back look. One that suits me better. I am now laid-back, happy-go-lucky Elle. At least I'm trying to be. I want fun clothes. I want comfortable clothes. I stop into almost every boutique on the little downtown strip and start building a playful, yet comfortable wardrobe. Turns out, to my delight, I'm a size smaller now, too. Stress will do that to you, I suppose. Things I never thought I could pull off before look amazing now. Maybe it's just my new outlook or maybe the one size down is the reason. Either way, I don't care. I'm having a blast trying everything on.

By the time I've finished shopping I am tired and starving. I head back to the cottage to unload my new things. Tonight I have dinner alone at a restaurant. I need to pick something that says I'm not on a date, and I'm not a pathetic woman eating alone. Needless to say I deliberate on this conundrum for a while.

I settle on a jean skirt, a green cotton tee, and a pair of wedge sandals. I grab my purse and stand at the door, knob in hand. *This better not end up sucking, Jenny.* I twist the knob, push the door ajar, and start walking. I wander up and down the main drag a few times, passing restaurants and trying to decide on which one. Some are just too fancy to eat at alone. Dimly lit, soft music playing, and couples hand-holding. Some are too loud and the crowd too young for my taste. The Pig Pit is where I end up. There is bluesy music drifting through the air and it's decorated in plain metal tables that have brushed steel tops. It's crowded but not loud or overwhelming.

"How many tonight?" the hostess asks.

"Just one," I reply, trying my best not to sound sad, lonely, or pathetic, like I feel.

"Right this way." She walks me to a small table in the corner at a window. I look at the menu and quickly decide on a pulled pork sandwich with all the fixings. The waiter comes, takes my order, and promises to return with my lemon water shortly.

As I sit there looking around, watching the other customers, I realize that no one is paying attention to me. I'm a ghost. I, however, notice all of them. There are some really interesting conversations. A group of college-aged guys are talking about a professor who apparently spits when he talks and therefore no one wants to sit in the front two rows. How spit can reach two rows back is baffling to me. I chuckle quietly to myself listening to their banter. The table to my back is involved in a much deeper conversation about God and His existence. I almost choke on my water as a woman counters her friend asking, "If God exists then what's up with the Holocaust?"

"Here you are." The waiter smiles as he puts my food down in front of me. "Enjoy."

"Thank you."

I put my napkin in my lap and dig in. My eyes dart around as I take small bites of my sandwich. There are a few guys at the bar who keep looking over here but besides that no one seems to notice that I am sitting alone eating. Plus, the three guys at the bar aren't ugly. I don't openly stare at them because I don't want to draw attention to myself but the quick glances that I do steal shows them all to be quite attractive. *Okay, maybe you were right...no one gives a shit. It's not so bad.* I don't feel like a leper. Yet.

By the time I finish quite possibly one of the best pulled pork sandwiches in history--what did they put in it anyways? Goat cheese, maybe--I am so stuffed I feel like I'm going to waddle home. The waiter brings me the check and after settling the bill I stand to make my way out.

"Hey," a voice calls. I ignore it because obviously they couldn't be talking to me. "Hey, excuse me." I stop and turn towards the voice. Two light blue eyes on a handsome face meet mine.

"Hello?" I ask.

"Would you like to join us for a drink?" he asks as he motions to the other two guys. I feel a smile creep over my face. They are hitting on me! "Um, thanks for the offer, but no," I retort.

"Oh come on, you don't look like you're in a rush. Just sit with us," Blue Eyes says.

"Why?"

"Why not?" he counters. I shrug, trying to come up with a reason, but the white noise and chatter of the restaurant distracts me.

"Okay, one beer." I give in and three good-looking men smile and point to the empty stool at the end of their row. Blue Eyes is clearly the outgoing one, tall and confident. He is now sitting furthest from me. In the middle sits a dark-haired stocky man who has a friendly face. Next to me is, I guess, the quiet one. He nods his head at me when I sit down and I can't figure it out but I'm intrigued at his quiet demeanor. He, like Blue Eyes, is tall and well built. The three of them are dressed casually but all look like they spend ten hours a day at a gym. Their shirts stretch tightly around their biceps and chests. The quiet one has light brown hair and the strangest hazel eyes I've ever seen. They're captivating. He hasn't said anything yet but I feel strangely connected to him, comforted in his presence.

"Ben," the outgoing one says.

"Hi Ben," I say, leaning forward to see him.

"John," the stocky middle guy shakes my hand. "Nice to meet you."

"Hey. I'm Elle," I say to the three of them.

"Colin. Hi," says the one with the hazel eyes, which lock on mine as he reaches his hand out to me. I shake it. The contact makes my body tingle like chemicals colliding. His eyes widen slightly as if he feels it too.

Whatever feeling it is startles me and I drop his hand. He only said hello but his eyes look like coming home. It takes me by surprise and I'm not prepared for it. Immediately I feel out of place. I don't want a beer. I feel panic coming on. I slide off my seat and stand nervously, shaking my head, with Colin's hazel eyes never leaving mine as he stares at me with curiosity.

"Sorry guys, but I think I need to head home, maybe another time. It was nice meeting you though," I sputter, excusing myself, and quickly dart out of the restaurant before they have a chance to say anything. *What is wrong with me, Jenny?*

Searsport is nice because from my cottage at the Inn I can walk anywhere I need to so far. My walk home gives me plenty of time to overanalyze why I bolted tonight. Dinner had gone well. I did it and I didn't feel strange or judged. In fact, it was nice to just sit alone and enjoy a meal. Why couldn't I enjoy the company of three good-looking guys over a simple beer? They weren't creepy or mean. All three were friendly. It was Colin's touch, his eyes. It was too intimate for two strangers and it threw me.

By the time I arrive home my mind is reeling. I can't get Colin or his hazel eyes out of my mind. They're unforgettable. I can't wrap my head around the fact that I felt so relaxed and at ease when his eyes were so intent on mine. Like we'd known each other our whole lives. Like he saw me. The electricity that rocketed through me when our hands touched was surreal, I shake the ridiculous thoughts from my head. I also didn't stay, I remind myself. I bolted like some crazy person with no explanation. I may not be crazy but I certainly acted crazy.

I fill a glass with water and sit on the deck watching the moonlight reflect off the ocean. The light undulates with the shift of the tide. It's breathtaking. *Okay, Jenny, one thing down. I miss your laugh tonight. I miss talking to you.* A breeze whips around me making me feel alive.

I switch on the kitchen radio and "Keep Hope Alive" fills the small open space. The Crystal Method reminds me of early high school. I turn it up as loud as I can and plop down on the couch. Leaning my head back on the cushion I close my eyes, take a deep breath, and smile, letting the electronic pull of the music lift me up. Hope creeps back into my soul. When it ends I stand and stride with purpose to the fridge and pause. I grab the sharpie in the pencil holder and cross out number one on my list. Done.

"That was odd, what the hell?" Ben hollers two seats over to me.

"Yeah seriously, what'd you do to her hand?" John asks.

"I have no idea." I shrug, still slightly stunned.

When she sat next to me I couldn't tear my eyes from her. Brown silky hair hanging at her shoulders and those eyes--I swear they cut right through me. Her eyes had flashed emerald sparks as she looked at me. She was stunning but not in the way that makes you intimidated like some women. She wasn't overly made up or trying too hard. There was a soft presence about her. I felt like I'd known her my whole life. Like she knew all my secrets just from touching my hand. She bolted before I could stop her and for a moment I wanted to run after her. I didn't, of course. That would probably scare the shit out of her. She seemed so delicate, maybe five- five, but fragile in some way. Her hourglass figure didn't go unnoticed. But something about the way she carried herself said that she had no idea how beautiful she was and that she was lost. A deep sensation that this was just the beginning washed over me. How ridiculous was that thought? I'd probably never see her again.

PRESENT

ELLE

DAY 2

The pitter-patter of raindrops lulls me out of a deep sleep. I crack my eyes open to a gray and gloomy room. The clock reads eight a.m. I groan, pulling the covers over my head and go back to sleep for another two hours.

"See a movie alone," the list reads. I'm not in the mood...It's such crappy weather out today that I just want to curl up on the couch with my Kindle in my jammies and read for the day. Maybe even nap. *I don't have to do something every single day really. Do I, Jenny?* I hold my breath and wait for an answer that never comes.

I drink my morning coffee sitting curled in one of the armchairs reading. I can feel that stupid list calling me. *Dammit, Jenny.* I set the kindle on the coffee table and pace around the room deliberating. Decisively I jump in the shower, resolving to get ready and see a movie. I throw on jeans, cowboy boots, and a lightweight long-sleeved shirt.

After putting on some mascara and lip gloss, I pull my hair haphazardly into a ponytail and set out.

I stop at the first shop I come to, buy an umbrella, and ask for directions to the nearest theater. The young lady at the register is stunning and perky. Even on this gloomy day she's a ray of sunshine. It makes me laugh as I step back out into the rain and start my three block walk to the theater.

It's small and old with a classic brick exterior reminiscent of a small town fifties theater. When I get to the ticket booth I stare up at the sign trying to figure out what's starting soon that'd I'd want to see.

"One for *Hit and Run*, please," I tell the kid working the booth.

The pimply kid behind the counter informs me that it will be eleven dollars which I promptly hand over to him in exchange for my ticket. I skip the concession stand, heading straight for theater number ten. I pick out a spot, just where I like, and sit. I tuck my umbrella under my seat with my purse and settle in.

The theater starts to fill up. People jostle up and down the narrow rows to claim their seats. No one sits in the seat to the left or right of me and no one asks me to scoot down a seat to make room for their party. I avoid all eye contact with people, not wanting to draw attention to myself. When the lights dim I'm relieved that all eyes are now focused on the screen and not scanning around the room.

The movie is pretty good. A former getaway driver jeopardizes his Witness Protection Plan identity in order to help his girlfriend get to Los Angeles. The Feds and his former gang chase them on the road. There are a lot of funny parts that make me laugh. When the lights finally come back up and the credits are rolling I stand and move into the shuffle of exiting movie goers. There are couples holding hands and talking quietly about their opinion of the movie, as well as groups of friends laughing over certain parts and quoting lines and a few other people who, like me, seem to be alone.

I thought maybe it would feel lonely to see a movie alone, that I would be sad not to share my opinion on it while leaving with someone. I'm not, though. It wasn't the best moment of my life but it was enjoyable and no one will disagree with my thoughts on it because there's no one to share my opinion with.

Did it, Jenny. One more step forward. Did you enjoy the movie? That whole scene about what happened in prison was pretty funny, yeah? "I was butt-f* * * * * by a Filipino dude, Okay!!! Solve your dilemma of what part of the world my ass traveled to?!?" Made me laugh, anyways. I wish you were here. You would have peed your pants over that one.

The rain has stopped, the clouds have broken and the sun's just starting to give up its fight for the day. I wander slowly back to the cottage, taking my time and watching people as they hurry in and out of shops. People don't seem to know how to slow down. They're all bustling towards their next errand or destination. I don't have worry about that. I have nothing to get home to. I could stay out all night long. I could stay in all day long. No one would care. It's a liberating feeling, really. I smile to myself as I turn left to the path leading to my cottage.

I dry off one of the patio chairs and sit with a glass of wine staring out over the ocean lost in thought. The warm summer breeze picks up and hazel eyes assault my thoughts. Who is Colin and why am I so pulled to him? How ridiculous. Chances are slim I'll run into him again. My fingers move over my palm where his hand clasped mine momentarily. I take a deep breath and push out of my chair. Maybe another glass of wine and making dinner will take my mind off of him.

I finished my protein shake for dinner and it's left me feeling less than satisfied. Even my workout and classes at the gym today did little to distract me. I wonder what she's doing right now. I can't get those green eyes, freckles, and a simple name out of my head. It seems like everything has changed. She's too old to be a college student, otherwise I might have walked around the local campus looking for her. I've never been so taken with someone just from exchanging hellos. I keep picturing her little button nose wrinkling up and her eyes going wide when our hands met. Whatever she felt scared her, but I felt it too, like a tug. No, that's not right, it was something more.

She unguarded me, her smile took me in and hooked me. When I'd tried to explain it to Ben later he laughed and said I was growing a vagina and just needed to get laid. Maybe he was right, but that doesn't explain the strange draw I feel to her, to find out more about her, to wrap my arms around her. I drag a hand down my face and shake the thoughts from my head. Grabbing a granola bar I crash onto the couch hoping something good will be on TV to distract me tonight.

PRESENT

DAY 3

I definitely drank too much wine last night. I woke up this morning sore from sleeping on the couch and the TV was still on. I don't even remember what I was watching when I fell asleep, I just remember the wine tasting delicious. My mouth is dry and my stomach is rolling in protest. I tried drinking some water but only got one good chug down before I thought I might throw up. I gave up any sort of productive ideas for the day and have been lying in bed reading for the last five hours, dozing in and out of sleep occasionally, but haven't gotten in the really good nap that I think I need.

At five I decide to finally roll out of bed and take a shower. I hope that will wake me up and make me feel better. By the time I finish in the bathroom I do feel more refreshed and awake but I'm also starving. I putz around the kitchen looking for something to make but am in serious need of hitting the grocery store. I really don't want to get dressed enough to eat out and I don't know any of the local delivery places so I throw on some yoga pants and a tee shirt and walk to the grocery store.

I skip the cart and grab a basket, I can't buy more than I can carry home anyways. After picking up some staples like pasta, sauce, bread, and tuna, I head to the produce section. I need to eat more fruits and veggies. My diet has seriously been lacking in healthy foods lately. Plus I have a kitchen again. I can cook and enjoy whatever meals I want! A smile creeps across my features at the thought. How pissed is Ryan right now, though?

"I felt it too," a deep masculine voice comes from behind me. Something familiar tugs at me. I ignore it, assuming he's talking to whoever he's shopping with. I continue picking up and squeezing avocados for ripeness. The man clears his throat and repeats, "I felt it too, Elle." I whip around, ripe avocado in hand, and come face to face with those amazing hazel eyes. The air in my lungs whooshes out of me before I can form words.

"I...excuse me?" I stutter. His eyes are trained on mine. I feel like I'm in a trance, frozen in my spot.

"When we shook hands. Whatever that feeling was. I felt it too." He leans against the tomato display, picks one up, and tosses it in the air once, then catching it. "I've been thinking about it ever since."

He's much taller than me: over six feet, and his tee shirt is tight across his broad shoulders, the muscles of his chest outlined by the thin fabric. His arms are rippled with muscles from his shoulders to his wrists. His narrow waist is highlighted by his drawstring running pants and his sneakers are untied. It makes me smile. I force myself to look back to his eyes. He's smirking at me and one lone dimple is etched in his face. His jaw line is strong and masculine. He's like an Abercrombie and Fitch model from the nineties all grown up.

"Elle?" His voice is so deep it sends a shiver through me.

"Sorry. I...ah, it's Colin right?"

"Yeah. Colin."

"I'm sorry about the other night. It was rude to just run off I guess." I guess? *Jenny, help me out here, I am seriously making an ass out of myself.*

"Was it me?" he asks. His face is warm and friendly. Inviting.

"No, of course not. I just don't hang out much with people. I'm kind of a loner," I lie. Well it's true of me now but I used to love hanging out with people. I also realize how pathetic this sounds and wish I could retract the statement.

"Oh, so you probably want me to leave you alone then," he says despondently. I instantly feel bad. I don't ever want to see this man frown again. *What is wrong with me, Jenny?* "No, please, did you want to finish shopping together?" I ask hopefully. I want him to say yes, but I know it's a bad idea. I should let him walk away. He shoots me a wary but hopeful look. "I'd love to." The smile he gives me right then sets my mind at ease and unleashes a jar of butterflies into my belly. He picks up his basket from the floor as I tell him the last few things I need.

"So kale, avocados, beets, carrots, apples, and lemons, huh?" he teases.

"I make a mean green juice, but the avocados are for sandwiches." His arm brushes mine as he reaches over me for a bag of baby carrots and I have to stifle my gasp at the contact.

"You eat pretty healthy. Do you work out?" he asks.

"I used to run. I haven't for a while, but I try to eat

clean. And no, I'm not a vegetarian or anything. I just eat as many fruits and veggies as I can when eating at home. Going out- all bets are off," I say with a smile.

He reaches for a package of steaks and tosses it in his basket. "I like meat and potatoes," he says, making a face, then pounds a fist on his chest. A laugh bursts out of me at his bad caveman impression. It surprises me. I haven't really laughed in such a long time. His eyes crinkle and he lets out a thunderous laugh. It's pure joy like a serenade and I instantly want to hear it again.

"So, what do you do?" I ask as we stand in the checkout line together.

"I'm a personal trainer and I teach boxing at my gym a couple blocks over."

"That's why you have so many muscles," I flirt. Why am I flirting?

"Have you been checking me out?" he teases. A blush creeps up my neck because I most certainly have. Who wouldn't?

"Maybe," I mumble.

"So what about you? What do you do?" he asks.

"Um, right now I'm on vacation. Renting one of those cottages at the Inn."

"That's nice. Where are you from?"

"Here. Searsport," I say nervously, wrinkling my nose. I don't want to talk about myself anymore. I don't want to answer questions.

"Did I say something wrong?" Colin asks, drawing his brows together.

"No! Of course not. I just don't like talking about myself very much."

"I thought we were trying to get to know each other," he says playfully.

"We were. I just...I don't know. I'm sorry, Colin," I trail off. His arm comes up, wrapping around my shoulder and he pulls me into his side. It's shocking. His touch, so casual yet affectionate. I don't even know him. I haven't been held this way, comforted by a man in so long, I'm stunned. "It's all right. We can avoid personal topics for now," he says quietly.

"Thanks," I murmur. He drops his arm as I move to unload some of my groceries onto the belt and I actually feel the loss of his touch. Impossible.

"Where are you parked? I'll walk you to your car." His voice fills the silence that's stretched between us.

"I walked here," I tell him.

"From the Inn?" He looks horrified.

"Yeah. It's not far. I like walking." I shrug.

"It's dark out, Elle, you can't walk home alone. Let me give you a lift."

"I really don't mind walking. It's no more than two miles." I stand firm. He stops and stares at me momentarily. "Fine, I'll walk with you then," he says.

"That's ridiculous! Then you have to walk back to your car, plus, what about your groceries?" I counter.

"I'll put the groceries in my car. Then I'll walk with you."

"Why are you doing this?"

"Why not?"

"That's not an answer," I huff.

"I'd like to make sure you get home safe." He sounds so sincere but it doesn't make any sense for him to be so nice to me. I'm out of ideas to get rid of him though.

"Fine. I'll let you drive," I say, finally giving in. A smug smile spreads across his face and that dimple pops out.

When we get to his car he pops the trunk and loads the groceries into it before opening my door for me.

"Thank you."

"For what?" he questions.

"Opening my door for me. That's sweet." I smile.

He shuts the door, rounds the car, and folds into the driver's seat. We pull out of the lot and head toward the Inn. "So what do you do for fun?" I say, venturing at small talk.

"Well, I like to read. I love concerts and music in general and boxing." He glances at me. "What about you?"

"Hmmm, chocolate. I love chocolate." I chuckle.

"You do chocolate for fun?" he laughs.

"Oh, right. Fun. I too read. A lot. I like movies, I love music, and exploring new places or trying new things."

"So you're adventurous," he states.

"Well, no I wouldn't say that, but I like experiencing new things," I explain. "That's me, number eleven." I point to my cozy cottage. He pulls the car to the side of the road and puts it in park.

"Well, Elle. It was nice running into you again," he says. His eyes are directed at mine.

"Yeah. Thanks for the ride," I reply, quickly averting my gaze. I could get lost in his eyes and I can't afford to do that right now. He hops out of the car, jogging around the hood to my side, and gets my door for me.

"Thanks, Colin." I grab my grocery bags and make the short walk down the path to the cottage door. When I put my bags down to maneuver my key into the lock I'm swung around into Colin's chest.

"Uh.. Colin?" My voice shakes slightly.

"I just need to know, Elle," he whispers.

One large hand wraps around the nape of my neck

while his other moves to the small of my back, startling me. Being in his arms has an intense and instant effect on me. He leans down, bringing his face to mine until our lips hover a whisper apart. I stare up into his eyes unmoving and unconsciously lick my bottom lip. Before I can blink his lips are on mine, hot and soft, exploring me. He nips my bottom lip, drawing it out a bit before I relent and push up on my tiptoes to deepen the kiss. My hands tangle in his hair without me telling them to and my torso pushes into his, wanting--needing--to be closer. The electric current that runs through my body is like nothing I've ever felt before. It's terrifying and exhilarating. The hand at my neck loosens slightly as our kiss goes from frantic passion to slow and sweet.

By the time he pulls his lips from mine I'm breathless and dizzy. We stare unmoving into each other's eyes and I swear a thousand conversations pass between us. It's surreal. He doesn't know a damn thing about me but right now I feel like I've known him my entire life. Not just known, loved. I bite my bottom lip and the guttural groan he lets out almost undoes me. He bends forward and kisses my forehead. All I can taste is this moment.

"What was that?"

"Everything," he breathes. "Elle, I need to see you again." His deep voice is raspy and gravelly and it does funny things to me. I sigh, knowing it's a bad idea, but find myself nodding my head anyways.

"All right," I whisper as my cheeks flush with heat.

He straightens up and grabs my grocery bags from the ground. I unlock the door to the cottage and we walk in together. I watch him curiously as he sets my bags on the counter and looks around. I find that I want him to know me. He moves to the fridge and stops.

"What's this?" He turns and cocks an eyebrow at me.

"A list," I reply sheepishly. It's pretty ridiculous to read through even to me sometimes. I watch as he picks up the Sharpie on the counter next to the fridge and blacks out "- Kiss a stranger." He turns and beams his brilliant smile at me. "I think you covered that one today," he smirks.

"Colin."

"Yes?"

"What did you need to know?" I ask.

"If kissing you would have the same effect as shaking your hand did." He struts over to me, stopping just shy of touching me.

"And?" I push.

"Even more so," he murmurs and takes my hand in his.

"I feel it too, but Colin, I don't understand it. It scares me a little," I say faintly.

"I don't know what it is, Elle, but I'm not stupid enough to let this go when I feel like my life started when I saw your face." I suck in a sharp breath. I feel the exact same way but I wasn't going to say it out loud.

"I have to get my groceries home but...can I see you tomorrow?" he asks.

"Okay," is all I can manage. He brushes a light kiss across my lips that leaves a trail of heat and want behind. He grabs the receipt from my grocery bag and writes something on it, places it on the counter, and comes back to me.

"Call me tomorrow." His arms come around me, tightly hugging me to his body. I wrap my arms around his waist and squeeze back. Home. It feels like home. Impossible.

He kisses the top of my head before pulling away. I walk him to the door and watch, completely dumbfounded at the events that just took place, as he gets in his car and drives away. When I get back to the kitchen I notice the receipt.

"*Incredible . Call me. 843-3327*"

I tack the note to the fridge and do a little happy dance. I feel giddy and breathless. *Jenny. Holy Crap, Pleaseeeee tell me you witnessed all that and please tell me it isn't too good to be true. I want to call you right now and talk all night about it.*

I put away the groceries, throw on a nightgown, and curl up in bed to read with a face-splitting smile. It's been too long since I've felt this much joy and it feels like my heart might crack from it.

I drive away from her house and I have the strangest feeling of peace. I don't even know her last name, yet I know down to my core that I will do anything she wants, anything she needs, anything she asks. I'm pulled, drawn to her. My gut tells me not to let her out of my sight, to take every second I have with her and make it count. It was torture having to leave.

What else could I do though? I couldn't very well tell her that I was staying. I don't want to scare her but these feelings taking over are so intense, and out of my control. If she doesn't call tomorrow, if I've scared her, I don't know what I'll do. Those lips. That kiss. It was pure fire. She tasted so good. Just a kiss. Makes me wonder what other things will be like. I liked the way she fit next to me. It was as if she was custom made for my body.

I pull into my parking space and wander to my apartment in a daze. Elle is the only thing I can focus on. Our conversation was easy, the banter playful. Is it possible to have an instant connection with someone? Because this feels like a hell of a lot more than lust. My brain forges on at a million miles a minute as I unload my groceries. What was that list on her fridge? Am I crazy? Who is she? How do I get to know her better? Why do I feel like an addict going through withdrawal? I think I *did* just grow a vagina. I crack open a beer and turn on ESPN where testosterone is king. I need to pull it together.

PAST

2011

If you're not careful life will rape you of anything beautiful. It can steal your hope. Devastate your soul. Kill your spirit. You could wind up like me, lifeless and trapped.

His blotchy, sweaty, bloated belly moves over me harshly jerking forward and backward. His kisses are slimy and sloppy and make me want to gag. I try not to visibly recoil from him. I don't, of course, because that would alert him to the fact that he disgusts me. I turn my head to the side, avoiding his kisses and eyes and silently pray that he finishes soon. There's no hope of me finishing. How could I? I'm actually repulsed by him. It wasn't always this way. I was attracted to him once. In the beginning he was loyal and kind. He made sure I knew that he'd never leave me.

Instead of gushing love and romance he'd tell me we're a good match. Never "I love you." No compliments. I missed the romance secretly, but figured as he grew emotionally over the years he'd become more affectionate and better at expressing feelings. I was twenty-five when we married, he was twenty-six, and we were young with plenty of time to grow together.

Expressing feelings did start to become easier for him after we married but they were feelings of animosity and rage. Lashing out at me verbally. Hateful words used to cut me down to size. Snide remarks about me and how disappointing and pathetic I was. I let it all slide for so long that eventually when I realized he was being abusive, it was too late to stick up for myself. At least I thought it was. I was so beaten down I didn't know who I was anymore. Words can cut things that are unseen. I started believing the bullshit he spewed at me. I am ugly. I am disappointing. I am lazy. I am bitchy. I am worthless. I offer no value in this life. I don't do anything right.

After a year or so he started with more violent stuff. Not hitting me, but when dinner wasn't up to his expectations, swiping his arm across the table and scattering the place settings and food onto me and the floor. He'd humiliate me, removing all the towels from the bathroom, forcing me to walk naked to the bedroom to get dressed or kicking the door open while I'm on the toilet. Twice he's thrown a glass at me but missed, thank God. I'm scared of him a lot. My fingertips are holding onto the cracks in our foundation, and I know that I should let go, but I can't.

When I was laid off from my job this year it was the last straw for him. Two weeks into my unemployment he laid into me. You are so fuckin' worthless, Elle, he would say. What are we going to do, live in poverty? Ha! *Poverty*. Hardly. He makes a decent salary and for any couple that should be enough to sustain us for a while until I find another job but apparently we were white trash now. I, of course, still contribute to the household: I have my hefty inheritance to fall back on. My inheritance is what we fight most about.

My parents' death had made headlines due to the tragic nature of the accident. I knew it would, hell, everyone knew who we were, my father was one of the most successful businessmen in the area. My sister and I threw a benefit to end drunk driving after their death. After the accident. My long blonde hair fell in silky sheets down my back and the evening gown I had on clung to my curves in a way that made men look. I stood with my sister shaking hands and thanking people for their support. That's where Ryan and I met. He'd looked dashing that night. He'd said all the right things and known all the right people. He dazzled me. We dated for a year and when he proposed I'd agreed, much to the dismay of Jenny.

I do everything I can think of to try and please him but nothing makes him happy. I try being extra good, loving and sweet. I try doing all the little things he likes. The only adjective he uses to describe anything is "tolerable." Nothing is ever wonderful or amazing...just tolerable. He is a miserable, angry, negative person. We fight frequently and although our arguments are never resolved he goes on acting as if things are fine. It's frustrating. I'm sensitive. I'm a feeler. I'm emotional. His way of life goes against every grain of my being. I want to talk things out. I want to feel things. It's been years of this now.

I live with a mean stranger who expects me to put out. It disgusts me but I give it to him without argument. If I'm lucky he's quick and I can go to sleep. People wonder how it happens. How you can be an independent, bright young woman and wind up in an abusive relationship. My home life must have been poor or I'm mental and think I deserve his treatment. We slid and slipped into this relationship. I didn't see it coming until it was too late. I had wonderful parents who were loving and encouraging to both my sister and I. My parents are probably rolling over in their graves right now.

PRESENT

DAY 4

I can hear knocking at the door but I'm in the shower. No one knocks at my door. I speed my shower along, hop out and wrap a towel around myself while shuffling towards the door. I open it and no one is there. Grumbling with irritation that I cut my morning shower short only to have missed whoever was at the door, I notice a small rectangular box near my feet. I bring it inside and put it on the counter. I'm not sure I want to open it. But only Colin knows I'm here so who else could it be from? I pull the lid off the box. Inside are two movie tickets and a note:

"Meet me tonight?"

The thoughtfulness of what he's just done takes my breath away. He's made it clear that he's vulnerable, something I'm not sure I can do. I pick up one of the movie tickets. *Searching For Sonny*. I have no idea what it's about but something tells me that he picked something he thought I would enjoy. I grab my prepaid cell which so far only has

Joe Jowett's number programmed in it and dial Colin's number.

"Hello?" he answers, breathing heavily, out of breath.

"Is this a bad time, Colin?" I ask.

"Elle?!"

"Yes," I answer.

"No, I was just working out." he says breathlessly.

"Why'd you answer your phone in the middle of a workout?"

"In case it was you calling." I can hear his smile through the phone.

"That sounds like a bad pickup line, you know that, right?" I tease.

"Did it work?"

"Well, I was calling to say that I'd like to see the movie, so I'll be there. I guess, yeah, it worked." I chuckle.

"Excellent! So, what's on your list today, Elle?" Surprised that he remembers or wants to know, I glance over at the list and scan down. "Start a conversation with a stranger," I answer.

"Hmm, so does ordering popcorn at the movies count?" he asks.

"No." I laugh. "More like, walk up to a random person and ask how their day is going or what they do for work. Something that would spark an actual conversation," I explain.

"What's up with this list anyways?" he prods.

"Maybe I'll explain it later, you should finish your workout."

"Okay. I'll see you tonight at seven then?"

"I'll be there." We both say goodbye at the same time, making things awkward for a moment, neither one of us wanting to hang up first. I end up hitting the Off button on my phone just to stop the insanity.

With that out of the way, I decide to head up to one of the little cafes that has outdoor seating and enjoy a coffee while picking out whom to start a conversation with. It's a gorgeous cloudless day out. I decide on a cute little coffee shop with some patio sets on the sidewalk called The Freaky Bean. I have my coffee in hand as I scan people passing by. A woman plops down at the table next to me, book and coffee in hand. When our eyes meet she gives me a small smile which I return. I watch as she sips her coffee and enjoys her book, completely oblivious to her surroundings. Her chin length blonde hair shines in the sun making it look like she has a halo. She periodically tucks a stray chunk of hair behind her ear as she reads.

"Excuse me?" I offer softly. Her head pops up. "What are you reading?"

The Life List." She holds the book up so I can see the cover.

"Is it good?" I ask.

"It's very good."

"Why?" My question seems to confuse or startle her, I can't tell which.

"It's real. It's true. It doesn't gloss over any of the harsh realities of life. I guess because it's brutally honest."

"Will you tell me what it's about?" I push.

"It's about a woman who thinks she has the life she's always wanted until she meets a stranger at a bar who...sparks her life light again. But she's married and has to make some seriously tough decisions. She has to find herself again. And, to do that, she has to hurt people she loves and herself a bit in the process. It's very moving." She pauses. "But she does it. Scary or not, she pushes through and takes control of her life, her happiness."

"It sounds fantastic. I might have to read it." I smile.

"I should finish it in the next few days... if you'd like, you could borrow it when I'm done. I come here every Friday morning." Her offer astounds me. Pure kindness. I'm a stranger and she's offering something to me for nothing, simply because I took the time to indulge her.

"I'd like that very much. Thank you. I'm Elle."

"Jenna. Nice to meet you." She sets her book down to shake my hand.

"Well, Jenna, I'm off, but I'll see you here next Friday?"

"It's a date." Her smile is warm and genuine and I feel a strange sense of accomplishment for taking the time to talk to her. Such a small act that resulted in unexpected happiness and kindness.

As I meander back to the cottage I wonder what my life would have been like if I hadn't met Ryan. Would I appreciate this list and the things on it still? The small things in life that free, happy people probably experience all the time. Maybe I wouldn't think to reach out and try these things because they would be common place, taken for granted. All I know is that this is my second chance at life and I'm living it to the fullest. I am not Ryan's prisoner anymore. I have no one to worry about but myself and my own happiness.

I walk up to the theater at six forty-five and Colin is already waiting for me. He's leaning against the brick exterior watching my approach. His gaze burns like a physical touch and my belly tightens in anticipation. Just the sight of him starts a fire blazing in the pit of my stomach. I smile, lifting my hand to wave, and his grin widens, exposing that sexy dimple.

"Elle," he says as he greets me. His voice has hoarseness to it. I can feel its rumble vibrate through me. His arm snakes around my waist and pulls me into a hug. I can feel every rock hard inch of him pressing into me.

"Hi Colin." I push out of his embrace slightly and look up to his handsome face.

"You ready?" he asks.

"Yes. Let's go." A hand slips to my lower back as he guides me into the theater. I reach into my pocket pulling out the tickets and hand them to him.

When we finally file into the theater he lets me pick where we sit and as we both settle into our seats he takes my hand and laces his fingers through mine. The contact seems so intimate. Gentle and kind and sweet. Emotions blow through me like a tornado. I'm not sure what I'm doing. I can't make a life with him. I'm married. I'm hiding until I can truly be free. I feel guilt for leading him on but I can't seem to tear my hand from his. I don't know why but I feel like I need him.

The movie's about three friends who find themselves suspects in a murder mystery at their ten-year high school reunion. Ironically, the events surrounding the disappearance of their friend, Sonny, is reminiscent of a high school play they once performed, coincidentally written by Sonny himself. It's light and funny and just right for a first date, a not-too-romantic and not-too-action flick. By the time it's over we're laughing and discussing which parts were best.

Colin is fantastic company. We walk back to his apartment which is close to the theater. It's neat and tidy which surprises me. His furniture is well worn and he swears it's the next thing on his list of things to purchase. He has matching plates, glasses, and silverware which, outside of the fact that he's actually decorated his apartment a bit, makes it even less of the bachelor pad than I was expecting. We spend the next four hours sitting on his couch talking about anything and everything. He loves animals, hates politics, is thirty-one, co-owns the gym he trains at, loves to read, listens to good music, and wants kids someday. He surprises me with his openness.

We share our dreams with each other. Our conversation happens naturally. His dreams are so similar to mine that I think he's fibbing just to keep us talking. But when I poke and prod him for details that come from really thinking about certain things you want out of life he has answers for them all. We talk about how lucky he is to work for himself and how that's what I strive to do someday. How much I love flowers and want to run a florist shop. He thinks it's a great idea. What it would be like to have kids. What kind of parents we hope to be. I tell him about wanting to own a small house on the beach someday because I love the sound of the water. He tells me that he's been saving for that for the last few years.

My gut occasionally clenches, telling me not to trust these feelings I'm inundated with. That Ryan too was easygoing in the beginning, but the further we venture in our conversation, the more my distrust slips away. We're snuggled on the couch together, the conversation quieting as we both grow tired. I'm wedged between his legs, his front to my back.

"So do you have any brothers? Sisters?" he asks softly. The question shouldn't surprise me but I wasn't prepared for it and I gasp.

"What?" he worries.

"Nothing. No. I don't have any family," I murmur quickly.

"Were you immaculately conceived?" he jokes.

"How funny," I say flatly. "And I was hoping for a battle of wits but you appear to be unarmed." His laugh fills the silence and brings a smile to my face.

"How about you?" I ask.

"Only child." He shrugs and yawns. "My parents live in Arizona."

"I should go. You're tired." His arms draw around my middle, squeezing gently as his head rests on my shoulder. "Stay," he breathes in my ear. A shiver starts at my neck and runs down through my legs. "We'll just sleep," he murmurs as if sensing my hesitation.

"All right." I nod my head once. His lips softly brush under my ear before I relax back into his chest. I let the tiny niggling of doubt fall away and close my eyes. Everything in this moment feels right and I decide to enjoy it. *Jenny, this is okay, right? God I wish you were here. What am I doing?*

PRESENT

ELLE

DAY 5

I'm cocooned in warmth and safety. Strong arms hold me tight. I'm nestled between long lean legs and resting against a broad chest that rises and falls steadily. Colin. I bolt upright wide-eyed looking over my shoulder where his eyes have now snapped open narrowing in on mine.

"Everything all right?" His voice is hoarse with sleep still.

"I...I just didn't know where I was for a second." I scoot a little further down the couch. He jackknifes up, snagging my waist and pulling me back to him. The sudden movement makes me flinch. His arms immediately let go and he positions me gently so we're facing each other.

"Elle, what was that? You cringed." He looks defeated. Hurt even. I let out a sigh wondering what to tell him.

"I'm sorry," I murmur.

"I'd never hurt you."

"I know that," I say disbelievingly.

"Do you?" he pushes.

"Colin..." My voice trails off.

"Yeah."

"I want to learn to fight. Will you train me?" I ask, changing the subject. He looks disgruntled for a moment and I wonder if this is it. This is the moment he says or does something nasty.

"Is that on your list, Elle?" he probes.

"Yes."

He's quiet for a moment. "Okay. Every morning, nine a.m., we train. Starting today," he says.

"Yeah? Really?" I clap my hands together in excitement and watch as his face goes soft and warm at my enthusiasm.

"Really. On one condition," he counters.

"What's that?" I ask skeptically.

"You have to trust me," he states firmly.

"Trust you how?"

"Completely," he says, his tone low and serious. "I want to know you, Elle, all of you." Desire burns bright in his hazel eyes but it's not just want that he's referring to. I pull in a deep breath to try and steady myself.

"I'll try. There's just...so much..." I don't finish my thought. I can't yet. His arms pull me snugly into his chest while his fingers trace small circles on my back. It's soothing.

"Okay," he whispers into my ear.

After stopping for coffee and taking me home to change, he takes me to his gym. It's no Planet Fitness, that's for sure. It's a boxer's gym. When we arrive there is only one other female in there and she's covered in tattoos. I definitely wouldn't mess with her. His friend John from the restaurant is behind the desk and I can see the other guy

Ben in the ring beating the ever-living crap out of someone else.

"Nice to see you again, Elle," John says and greets me with a warm smile.

"Hi. Thanks."

"Elle needs to fill out paperwork. I'm going to train her," Colin informs him.

"Oh yeah? Gonna learn to box a little?" he teases.

"I hope so." I suddenly feel nervous and reserved, like all eyes are on me.

John shuffles some stuff around under the desk before pulling out a clipboard with an information and waiver form on it and handing it to me. "Fill this out and just leave it on the desk when you're done."

"Okay."

"Elle, I'm going to hit the locker room, I'll meet you over at the bag whenever you're ready," Colin says, pointing to a punching bag in the back corner. I nod my head and find a chair to start filling out the paperwork.

Name, Address, Occupation, Marital Status, Previous Injuries. Panic flares low in my belly. I don't want to lie but I'm not sure what to put on the form that won't spark questions. He asked me to trust him. I decide to just put the truth down, well, almost: I check "Single" under Marital Status. He probably won't look it over anyways. When I finish I set the clipboard down on the desk and walk over to the bag.

A few moments later Colin comes out of the locker room, hits the desk tagging the clipboard, and then meets me at the bag. I watch as his eyes scan the answers written on the page, his brows furrowing when he gets to the Injuries section. His eyes come to mine.

"Jesus, Elle, it looks like the left side of your body was

crushed. What happened?" His face shows genuine concern.

"Um, me versus tree. Tree one, me zero," I jest. His concern doesn't lift.

"How much physical therapy?"

"I had enough, I promise. I have pins and plates too. I'm bionic." I'm trying like hell to keep this lighthearted but I'm not sure it's working.

"How long ago was the accident? I don't want to push you too hard and cause any injuries."

"Eight months ago."

"That's not a lot of time even with physical therapy." I look to him feeling deflated but hoping it doesn't show in my eyes.

"So, can I not learn?" I ask.

"We can, I just want to take it slow and I want you to tell me if anything at all bothers you," he instructs firmly.

"I promise!"

For the next fifteen minutes we stretch and warm up. He keeps babbling on about how important it will be for me to really stretch before and after workouts because of my injuries. I've heard it all before from the PT at the hospital but I keep that to myself. I'm more focused on watching him. The way his muscles flex, contract, and relax as he stretches and moves. His arms are massive and the plain white tank clings to his chest and stomach leaving little to the imagination. I already feel a light sheen of sweat coating me as he reaches for the tape. "Take off your sweatshirt before I tape your hands," he says. I glance down at my lightweight zip up sweatshirt. All I have under it is my sports bra. It's a full coverage sports bra, but still.

"Ah. Do I have to?"

"The sleeves will get in the way. I want to be able to see

your form and correct it if needed," he explains. I hesitantly start to unzip my sweatshirt. When the zipper gets halfway down I hear a sharp intake of breath and my eyes dart to his face just as his hand comes to rest on mine, stopping me from unzipping further.

"Elle, don't you have a tank top or something?" His eyes hazel eyes are ablaze and trained on my stomach. Heat flares low in my belly.

"It's too hot for both," I shrug. He quickly looks away mumbling something under his breath before disappearing into the locker room. When he comes back he places a wife beater in my hands.

"Change into this." He nods to the locker room door. I do as I'm told and quickly throw on his tank top. It's fitted in the chest but runs long, hitting me mid-thigh.

"Better?" I ask as I approach him. His eyes scan me top to toe not bothering to conceal the desire behind them.

"Mostly," he smirks. He reaches out, tagging my hand, and starts taping it. I watch his hands move efficiently over mine. Skin grazing skin, fingers skimming mine. When he finishes he moves to my other hand and repeats the process.

"Have you ever hit a bag before?" he questions. I shake my head no. He takes my right hand, turning it palm up.

"All right, first tuck, your four fingers, not including your thumb, into the first crease of your hand." He moves my fingers into position. "Bring your hand into a tighter fist, so your nails touch your palm." I nod, doing as I'm told. "Good. Now tuck your thumb over the front of your fingers, right under the joint. That's it. Now when you strike the bag try to hit with the first two knuckles only. Don't change your fist position, only your elbow and shoulders should move."

He moves behind the bag and instructs me to hit it.

When I do it barely moves and I feel like my hand exploded on impact. I wince in pain. Not what I expected. I wanted to feel powerful but all I feel is stupid.

"It's all right, Elle. Here, let's try something else." He moves behind me. "Put your left foot forward and your right foot back," he says as his hands come to my hips and he positions me. I can't focus with his fingers grazing my waist and I'm suddenly thankful for the thin fabric of the tank top. "Keep your knees bent and put your fists up, leading with your left," he murmurs low in my ear, making me tremble. He smells delicious. His hands leave my waist and come to my wrists. He tucks his front into my back and moves us as one, guiding me through the punch as he instructs. "Push off a bit with your back leg. As you extend your arm and fist, swivel your torso so that your fist isn't leading and your torso is driving your arm." My right fist connects with the bag again with his arm on top of mine as he controls the motion. The bag sways slightly under the force of my hit. "Feel the difference?" he asks. A finger trails down the scar on the back of my left arm as he steps back but he says nothing. I can't seem to concentrate with him touching me.

"Yeah I think so," I say. He moves behind the bag again and tells me to try it again, on my own. Once I've got the hang of it we move on to jabs, crosses, and hooks. I'm sweating like a pig by the end of our forty-five minute session together. He's encouraging the whole time. Always positive and helpful. I actually feel a sense of accomplishment by the time we're done. I feel proud.

"Nice job today!" John calls over to me.

"Yeah, Elle, lookin' good!" Ben laughs.

"Gee thanks guys," I laugh along with them. "I had fun. Thanks, Colin." He puts his hand on the small of my back and leads us to the entrance. "Will you come back tomorrow for more?" he prompts.

"Definitely!"

"Okay then. I'll see you tomorrow, at nine," he smiles.

"Nine then." Our eyes lock for an awkward moment as we wonder how to say goodbye. "Well. See ya," I say, turning on my heel. I push out the doors onto the busy sidewalk and want to kick myself. *That was really lame, wasn't it, Jenny? What am I doing?*

The walk home is peaceful and quiet and gives me plenty of time to think. I can't figure out the draw I feel to Colin. I've never felt anything like it before. I find myself wondering what he's doing right now and if he's thinking about me too. I have the most ridiculous urge to call him just to hear his voice. Even before Ryan I never experienced something like this. When he looks at me I feel beautiful, I feel safe. I can't really afford to trust anyone but my lawyer or to get involved with anyone but Colin makes me forget all that. He makes me want a life I'm not sure I can have. *Jenny, please give me a sign, something, anything. Am I allowed to have this?*

PAST

2011

I hate it when he's home with me because I never know how the day will go. Like if I'll make him angry or not. I live for work hours when I can happily pursue my life without ridicule or teasing or destruction of property meant to make me feel inferior. I don't know what will set him off. If I make the wrong breakfast it could end up dumped all over me. If lunch isn't to his liking plates could be thrown and smashed. If I'm not dressed right I will be screamed at and degraded.

My sister, thank god, is my lifeline. She's been asking me to leave him for years but the disgrace, stigma, and obligation that comes with marriage and divorce keeps me where I am. My soul rots and degrades more each passing day. She begged me not to marry him in the first place. She said something was off. He wasn't quite right. She said he had mean eyes. The more he pushed, the more pathetic I became. I grew pliant, eating from his palm, jumping when he said jump. Just as he had conditioned me, I feared him, yet still never allowed him access to the damned money he wanted to badly.

I used to be a happy person. A person with a sparkle in her eye. I was carefree, easygoing, fun, and knew joy on a regular basis. I'm smart. I have a college degree from a good school. I've built a career from my degree and I'm good at it. I had friends. Lots of good friends. I used to go out. I was passionate about life and love and myself.

None of that person exists anymore. She's been stripped of all redeeming qualities. My friends still occasionally try but they just don't like the way he treats me or that I put up with it. They don't understand why I don't just leave. They don't understand because they only hear him, but they've never seen the hot chili thrown at me because it was not to his liking, they've never seen him pick up my plate and hurl it across the room, screaming. They've never seen me scared and cowering from him. If I left would he take it further?

I daydream about leaving him all the time, but don't, because what would I tell people? He's not really done anything wrong. He's never hit me directly. He's not cheated on me that I know of, although I have my suspicions. He's a hard worker. He just tells me with actions and words at least twice a day how pathetic and disappointing I am.

His touch makes me cringe and I harbor so much resentment towards him that I don't like looking at him anymore. He sits on his couch, eyes glued to the TV, ignoring me, beer in hand from the time he arrives home until we go to bed. There is no partnership between us, I am responsible entirely for our household, and he gets to live in it. It's odd, really: six years ago I never would have put up with this kind of behavior. I would have been appalled. I certainly wouldn't have rolled over and just taken the shit he dishes out. I honestly don't know when or why or what it is about him that makes me take it.

If it wasn't for my sister, I'd have nothing. She is the only joy left in my life. She loves me no matter what. She is my rock. My confidant. My only family and my best friend. We can have entire conversations without actually speaking. Luckily my husband doesn't seem to care about us spending time together...as long as his dinner's on the table when he gets home and his lunch for the next day is packed. I spend as much time as possible with her to escape my marriage. She gives me glimpses of the old me back. She makes my soul feel light again.

At thirty, I'm afraid I won't find a better man so I lie and tell myself I'm in love with him. I will die sad and unhappy but married for years and years and he will think he lived a good life, a happy life. It's unfortunate sure, but I resigned myself to the truth of the situation a long time ago. I know at some point his rage won't stop at inanimate objects, that it will turn towards me, but what can I do, really?

Our fifth wedding anniversary is coming up this month and I dread the plans he's made. I will be expected to look nice, smile, and exude happiness during whatever we do. This could be simply a night out or an entire weekend away. If my skirt is too short or I look too nice he will make a comment and I'll have to change. If I don't want to put out he will try extra hard at foreplay after I say no repeatedly, which actually turns me off and dries me out even more than if he skips it all together. If I want to relax and do something I enjoy, like swim or read, it will become an issue of me ignoring and neglecting him. I can't win with him so I just don't try anymore. I wait for him to instruct me and follow orders, hoping that it doesn't result in screaming or a mess.

Fuck off.

    I can see your cooter in that skirt.

    Do something with me.

    Get a fuckin' job.

    Why isn't the house clean?

    Stop spending my money.

    Why are you such a bitch?

    Why can't you cook?

    You're being cunty.

    You're getting fat. Again.

    Why can't you do anything right?

    That shirt barely covers your tits, slut.

    Those shoes make you look trashy.

    I threw up last night when I got in...clean it up.

    You disgust me.

    You're worthless."

He treats me as if I'm simply a piece of trash that can be discarded at any time. There is no silver lining in life. He's a one-upper: if you had a bad day, his was worse. If you're sick, he's sicker. I've never seen the man give change to a homeless person, hold a door open, or give up his seat for someone. He's never done anything that normal people just do because it's what people do. There is no kindness. You'd think that by now I'd be hooked on booze and pills or some shit like that but surprisingly I'm too resilient for all that. I still have hope. Things will get better...they have too, right? I mean it's not a crime to hope that your husband will change. It might be completely stupid and naive but it's not a crime. What if I leave him and then he gets it and changes? I'd be alone and he'd be cured and move on with some young thing and treat her like gold.

When he drinks heavily, it's a different story. I contemplate leaving without a damned thing but the clothes on my back. He's extra nasty when he drinks and extra horny. I hate the way he smells and the permanent sneer that resides on his face as long as there's a beer in his hand. He makes lewd jokes that he thinks are hilarious but are offensive. He gropes me openly and it's embarrassing. If we're in public I have to pretend to be too intoxicated to notice his awful behavior. It's a wonder he hasn't been in a drunken brawl yet.

He also drives drunk. I try to convince him to let me drive but sometimes it just starts a bigger fight between us. My life over the last four years with him has become a shit storm so thick that I can't see my way out. He loves me. I know he does. He loves me the only way he knows how and it would wreck him if I left him. Still, it's not enough to stay, I know, but I do anyways.

He's that guy who torments little kids and finds it amusing. Kicks dogs when no one's looking or tosses a cat harshly. The guy with no filter who tells raunchy jokes and doesn't understand when no one laughs. The passive-aggressive guy whose mean, cutting remarks are masked in teasing so that others think he's funny. The guy who will pick up the pot of soup on the stove and dump it on the floor or you after claiming it tastes like shit. I have small burn marks from where it splattered still.

It's exhausting, really, living with it. Excusing it. Overlooking it. Tolerating it.

PRESENT

DAY 6

I wake up early, giving myself enough time to eat and get ready before I'm due at the gym. My nerves are on edge. One part of me can't wait to see him again but another part keeps reminding me that I'm not prepared to have a connection with someone. My only goal was to escape Ryan and attempt to accomplish my list. I don't know how long it will last, if Ryan's still looking for me or if I'm caught what will come of it. Everything's up in the air. Emotions swirl around inside of me but the one that keeps coming to the forefront is that I want to trust Colin. I want him to know me.

"Back for more," John greets me when I enter the gym.

"Yup. Can't seem to stay away," I tease.

"Colin's waiting for you." He nods in Colin's direction. The man never fails to take my breath away. He's seated on the mat by the bag we were at yesterday, an ear-to-ear grin on his face. His hazel eyes burn into mine as I make my way over to him.

"Morning," I say shyly.

"Morning. Glad you came back."

"I told you I would."

"Yeah well...I wasn't a hundred percent convinced you would," he says honestly.

I sit next to him on the mat and start stretching, every once in a while glancing up and catching him staring at me.

"What?" I ask finally.

He shakes his head and smiles coyly. "I just can't seem to take my eyes off you." The blush that crawls up my neck tells me my face must be bright red.

"Ready?" he asks, smirking.

"Yes." He pulls me up by the hand and tapes my wrists, his fingers lingering when he's finished.

"I want to work on combinations today," he tells me.

For the next hour I perfect my jab, cross, and hook until sweat is dripping down my back. By the time I'm out of the locker room and feeling a little less swampy I've decided to ask Colin over for dinner. For some reason I'm feeling bold. He walks me to the door, hand at the small of my back as always.

"See you tomorrow, same time?" he asks hopefully.

"Actually, I was wondering if you'd like to have dinner with me tonight." I keep my eyes trained on his shoes. Two fingers come to my chin, lifting it to his face.

"I'd love to," he says softly. I try to keep my face-splitting smile from emerging but it's a lost cause.

"Really?"

"Elle, I told you I wanted to get to know you. I meant it," he states. "What time should I come over?" His dimple makes a brief appearance, making the thoughts in my head jumble.

"Ah...right...can you come for six? I'd like to cook you dinner," I tell him. His eyes sparkle as his fingers drift from my chin to my jaw, resting just behind my ear. He sweeps the pad of his thumb over the apple of my cheek and says, "I'll be there."

I am a complete spaz all afternoon. I clean the cottage like a maniac even though there really isn't anything to clean. I talk to Jenny like she's there making fun of me for being neurotic. I spend two hours in the grocery store debating over what to make and changing my mind four times before settling on steaks, a goat cheese salad with fruit, and green beans. By the time I'm home and finished marinating the steaks my focus shifts to what I should wear. I don't have a lot of options and I'm out of time to go shopping. Everything I own is on the bed spread out as I repeatedly hold things up and look in the mirror before tossing them back on the bed. Eventually I settle on a jean skirt, black and tan cowboy boots, and a cowl neck tank top. It looks nice but not too nice.

I'm in the kitchen steaming the green beans when he knocks at the door. The clock reads five fifty-five. I smile. As I open the door my breath catches. He's in a crisp white button down shirt and jeans that hug him perfectly. His short brown hair looks like he's been running his hand through it. One hand bears an arrangement of flowers and the other a bottle of wine.

"Hi."

"Hi." We stand staring at each other, both fidgeting.

"Come in," I say, breaking the silence. He follows me into the kitchen and hands me the flowers.

"These are beautiful. Thank you." I pull a tall glass from the cabinet, fill it with water and place the flowers in it.

"How was the rest of your day?" he asks.

"Oh you know..." I trail off, trying to think of something

to say that doesn't give away that I spent my afternoon completely panicked about tonight.

"Nope. I don't," he chuckles at me.

"I went to the grocery store and then cleaned up a little," I divulge reluctantly.

"Would you like a glass of wine?" he offers.

"I'd love one." I pull out two wine glasses, a corkscrew, and hand them to him. Our fingers brush in the process sending a bolt of electricity straight between my legs. I put the finishing touches on the salad as he opens and pours the wine. I can't help but gape at his attractiveness as I steal glances at him wondering how his skin would feel under mine and how I would feel touching it.

"I thought we could eat out on the deck. It's so nice out." I take a swig from my glass letting the wine slide smoothly down my throat, hoping that it will calm my nerves.

"How can I help?" he asks. I already have the table set so we fix our plates in the kitchen and carry them out to the deck.

"This is a great view," he says as the sun sparkles against the ocean. I sigh, a slight smile playing on my lips. "I know, I love it here. It's been so peaceful."

"How long are you here?"

"I rented the cottage for a month."

"That's a long vacation."

"I guess."

"Where do you live?" he asks before taking a bite of steak. A groan bubbles out of him. "What did you do to this? It's amazing," he gushes.

"You like it?" I can't hide my astonishment. My cooking has been a source of tension for so long I just expected him to pick apart how awful it was.

"Like it? Elle, my mouth is watering. Seriously. Everything is amazing." His compliment makes me blush. "So, like I was saying. After your month is up, where do you go back to? Where's home?" I fidget nervously, debating silently if I should tell him the truth.

"I don't know. I don't know what I'm doing when my rental is up." It's the truth. I haven't thought that far ahead. He cocks an eyebrow at me.

"There's something you aren't telling me." It's not a question. He knows I'm hiding something.

"My sister died," I blurt. "She was my only family, my parents passed away years ago. I just needed to get away. I don't know what I'm doing after this. I haven't thought about it." His eyes are so intense they scare me. They're full of compassion and empathy. He looks pained almost, like he wants nothing more than to take my pain away.

"I'm so sorry, Elle," he croaks.

"It's okay. I mean, I'm okay. Now. Sorta." I'm rambling and I can't seem to stop. "But I didn't plan on you. I can't make sense of why I'm drawn to you. I know I shouldn't be because I'm shattered. Cracked. Broken," I whisper, ashamed. He moves his seat next to mine and wraps an arm around me, pulling me tight into him. What he says next shocks me to my core. "Cracked can be repaired. Filled in. Shattered can't. You might be cracked, Elle, but you're not beyond repair."

I lift my face to his slowly and push my lips into his. He immediately responds, deepening the kiss. My world's instantly set in perfect motion as he slides me onto his lap and wraps an arm around my waist while the other hand snakes through my hair. He kisses me until I'm breathless and panting. I pull away, gasping for air. His forehead rests on mine as we both catch our breath.

"What are you doing to me?" he rasps and right then I know that I can't give him up.

We finish dinner, Colin continues to gush over the food which still makes me blush and we retire to the living room after cleaning everything up. "More wine?" he asks. "Sure." I hand my glass out to him and watch as he strides into the kitchen to fill our glasses again. When he shuts the fridge door he pauses. I watch as he pulls the list from the fridge and carries it back in with our wine.

"Tell me about this." He places the list between us on the couch.

"My sister and I used to think up wild things that we would never dare to do...or that might be socially unacceptable. Those were some of the things we talked about. I want to try and do one every day," I finish in a hushed tone. I feel silly explaining it to him.

"Do you trust me?" he asks. I look to his face searching for a reason to not trust him but come up empty.

"I do." He snags a pen from the coffee table and crosses out learn to fight and trust someone. I can feel tears prick the back of my eyes. When he looks back to me he says, "Then tell me the rest."

I can't help it. I tell him everything about Ryan and the way he treated me. It rushes out of me. The pain, the hurt, the abuse. Humiliation fills my cheeks. I tell him everything right up until the moment after Ryan smacked me before noticing he'd drifted closer, the side of his thigh pressing against mine. "So after being degraded for so long, when he finally hit me...actually hit me.... I don't know... I snapped. My sister had just passed away and losing her broke me. I just remember thinking -run, so I did. He could still be looking for me." I shudder at the thought and stop there. He's holding me tightly in his arms now and I've never felt so safe or wanted in my life. I sniffle and clear my throat.

"Colin."

"Yeah." His deep voice at my ear sends chills through me.

"I have a lawyer. Joe Jowett. If anything happens to me. If Ryan finds me I need you to call him and tell him to put everything in motion. Can you do that?" I ask, still feeling embarrassed.

"I'll do anything you want." His voice is so sincere. So honest, it almost breaks me. I don't deserve him.

"Keep this in your wallet," I say, handing him Joe's card. I can feel unshed tears pricking the backs of my eyes. I pick up my phone and go outside for a moment to call Joe. I leave him a voicemail telling him that if he gets a call from Colin to put everything into action. I give him Colin's phone number and let him know that he can be trusted with all the information if necessary. If that time comes.

***

I leisurely trail my fingers up and down her arms as we lay on the couch together watching a movie. She's so responsive to my touch it drives me insane. I want to do more to her. I want to taste her, feel her, be inside her. But I can't. Not yet. It has to be her move.

When she told me about her husband, the things he did to her, said to her, rage made my vision blur. My jaw aches now from how hard I had clenched my teeth together. The thought of someone hurting her makes me sick. How could anyone treat her like that? She's so kind, small, quiet but vibrant. My instinct to protect has been pushed into over-drive. Her small delicate fingers toy with the hem of my shirt absentmindedly, occasionally making contact with my skin and leaving a trail of fire in their wake. The erection I'm sporting can't be hidden but she doesn't seem to notice or mind.

"Elle," I whisper into her ear.

"Mmm." She sounds sleepy. Content.

"Let me finish the list with you."

"What?" She perks up.

"I want to do the rest of the things on the list with you," I say again.

"Really?"

"Really." Her fingers stop moving and she inhales deeply.

"Okay," she lets out. "Colin." Her voice is breathy.

"Yeah."

"I'm tired from all the weight. I'm tired... of being strong. Will you stay the night and just let me lay in your arms?" She sounds like she's waiting for rejection. I tag the remote and hit the Power button, shutting off the TV before scooping her up in my arms and carrying her to the bedroom. Her little squeal makes me want to do more than just lay with her. Her smile, so beautiful.

I stand her up and finger the button on her jean skirt until it's undone. She lets it slide off her hips to the floor. Crossing her arms across her ribs she gathers the hem of her tank in her hands and slowly pulls it up and over her head, leaving her standing in only her bra and panties. The moon-light drifting through the window casts a shadow over her face but I can see the heat in her eyes as she reaches out to my waist, undoing my jeans and pushing them easily down my legs. Her fingers tremble as she works at the buttons of my shirt. I watch as her eyes go wide when my shirt hits the ground leaving me standing in my boxers, her eyes blazing as they come back to mine. She trails her fingers lightly over every ridge of my stomach, making me tense. My muscles twitch as her hands move over them.

She turns to pull back the covers and the dim light shows a ragged scar running down the back of her left arm and another from her left hip to her calf. My hands clench into fists at my sides wondering if there really was a car accident or if her asshole husband did that to her.

When she tucks herself into the bed and looks up at me all my rage subsides. She's stunning. Her brown hair frames her delicate face and the moon lights her creamy skin. Her bright green eyes glisten with unshed tears. I crawl in next to her and pull the covers over us. I slide my arm under the heavy fall of her hair and she puts her head in the crook of my arm, her face resting on my chest. Her fingers move in no particular pattern over the muscles of my stomach and back up over my ribs. Trailing and teasing. I pull her close to me and kiss her forehead, letting my hand skate over her hip to her stomach. She whimpers softly but I don't push anything further. I wait until her breathing is low and even before letting myself find sleep.

PAST

When I was a little girl I always thought I would end up with the hero. The strong, handsome man who swept me off my feet, loved and pampered me until I died from a full heart. I would be adored. The affection and love rolling off my man would make other women swoon and he would only have eyes for me. He'd also be the man in bed. I'd be perpetually wet and dripping with sex. He'd take great pleasure in giving me pleasure and because of that I'd be all too happy to please him as well. Orgasm would be my middle name.

None of that came true though. I've condemned myself to a life with an abuser who is average in looks, terrible in bed, and definitely never pampers or adores me. I haven't had an orgasm in years. Years! When he tells me tonight that dinner could have been better (if he had cooked it, of course, but he doesn't--ever), I'll nicely ask him how it could be improved, in his opinion, and next time I make it, take what he prefers into consideration.

When he sticks his fat slimy tongue in my mouth at bedtime I'll take it and pretend to like it. When his hairy heavy body shifts over mine, I'll moan at all the appropriate times until he's done. He's never gentle. Rough and fast, pounding into me without concern.

The absolute worst though is when he wants to snuggle. He crawls into bed and I pretend to be asleep. He rolls into me, pressing his front to my back, spooning me. His arm comes over my waist and pulls me to him. I hate the skin on skin contact. I hate the weight of his arm. I hate that he thinks we can have anything so intimate happen between us after listening to him tear me apart and throw things around, destroying them. It makes my skin crawl. I try not to cringe but sometimes I can't help it.

My only real reprieve is sleep. When I sleep I dream. I dream of something better, someone better, someone worthwhile, someone who loves me because they think I'm wonderful and beautiful and a good person. Sometimes I just dream of being alone. Content to live my life any way I see fit, devoid of screaming and hate and destruction. I love to dream.

I think terrible things. I wish him dead. I hope and pray that he will attempt to drive home drunk one night, get in a terrible accident, and die. Not a slow gory death, but a quick painless one. I don't want him to suffer. I just want to be free of him. Maybe his heart gives out and he just drops to the floor at work and by the time they call me it's just to tell me that it's too late... there was nothing they could do. I'm not so lucky though. If I'm going to escape him it will have to be me leaving him. My doing. I'm just not ready yet. I'll leave. I will. Jenny will make me. Jenny, my sister, my savior, my rock, my everything.

It takes several months but she's finally convinced me that it is the right time and that I have nothing to worry about because she will help keep me safe. It's coming. I want it. I just have to, you know, do it. His gambling started out innocently enough at first. Poker nights with friends or co-workers but now it's casinos and private games. He's constantly badgering me for more money. Money that I won't give him. Money that was left to me from my parents. They worked hard to earn that money and I won't let him gamble it away. He checks my computer and voicemail regularly to keep tabs on what I'm doing. I wasn't shocked to find out that he had found out Jenny convinced me to leave him. I was shocked and enraged that he had stormed to Jenny's apartment a few days later and told her she could fuck off and butt out of my marriage. A week later I found an email to some guy named Mitch. He advertised himself as a personal investigator. I couldn't believe Ryan would take things so far as to have me followed.

The day it happened I was sitting at home revamping my resume and my cell rang. I had no idea who the number belonged to. I usually don't answer calls where I don't recognize the number on the ID but my gut told me to pick it up.

"Is this Elle?"

"Yes, speaking."

"Elle, this is St. Mary's. Can you confirm that a Miss Jennifer Parks is your sister?"

"Yes ...what's this about? Is she okay?"

"Ma'am, we need you to come to St. Mary's as soon as possible. She's been in an accident."

"Is she all right?!" I shout in frustration.

"That's all the information I can give you. Someone will be here to discuss details with you when you arrive."

I don't remember leaving the house and driving to the hospital. But, when I arrived at the ER entrance, I left the car running and sprinted inside, screaming Jenny's name while squinting my eyes so I could see through my tears. A nurse, I think, placed her hand on my arm and led me to a room at the end of a long hallway. A doctor came in and I immediately assaulted him with questions.

"Please Mrs. Parks, calm down."

"It's Mrs. Darling.... please tell me what's going on!"

"Mrs. Darling, your sister, Jennifer had you listed as her emergency contact. She was in a car accident this afternoon. We did all we could but she didn't survive. We need you to identify the body and if you want, take her personal effects."

His words are garbled sounding. Why doesn't she look upset? Dead? Did he say dead? Dead as in she's gone? She can't be gone. I talked to her yesterday. She's all I have. Without her I have nothing, I am nothing. I. Am. Nothing. My face is wet and the doctor's mouth is still moving but I'm not hearing anything.

"Mrs. Darling? Mrs. Darling? Are you ready?" I squeeze my eyes open and shut a few times trying to get my bearing.

Cold. Numb. Dead. I feel what Jenny's been reduced too. I follow the doctor to the morgue and do what needs to be done. It feels like an out-of-body experience. I'm not really there. I'm watching myself. Elle Darling is a skin and hair shell, housing a soulless, spiritless person. I'm out of hope. I collapse outside on the sidewalk. Crumble and shatter, the pieces of me scattering and blowing in the breeze. The valet attendant comes to my side and asks if there's someone he can call for me. I manage to rattle off my husband's cell number. He tells me that my husband will be here shortly.

Ryan arrives and sits next to me on the bench. "I'm so sorry, Elle." He puts one arm around me. That's it. That is all the comfort I get. He doesn't wipe my tears away. He doesn't cry with me. He doesn't hold me close and offer support. "Let's go. It's cold out here," he says with no concern for me. No matter that I'm shattered. Devastated.

He tells me we can get my car later and I let him lead me to the car. I'm shaking uncontrollably and the tears refuse to stop pouring from my eyes. Ryan has the local alternative station turned up on the radio and continues to listen to it the entire drive back to our house, singing along to songs he knows. It grates on my nerves. I lost my sister. I just lost my sister and he's listening to music? I want to punch his face. I want to scream at him. I want to open the car door and throw myself out. None of these things happen of course.

When we get home I dart to the bathroom, take a sleeping pill, and then head to bed. "What are you doing, Elle? What about dinner?"

"Fuck dinner, Ryan!" snaps out like a verbal backhand across the face and I sink into our bed, pull the covers over my head and hope like hell that sleep will find me.

The next few days are terrible. The worst of my life. Ryan takes his three bereavement days off of work to be home with me. He sits at his laptop in the office doing god knows what or fucks around on Facebook. He does not help me plan my Jenny's funeral. He does not comfort me. He does not help me write the obituary or make phone calls to let people know what's happened. He just took three days to have time off and I hate him for it.

I, on the other hand, have been running around like a chicken with my head cut off. There is so much to do. So much to take care of. On top of the obligations, there is an elephant sitting on my chest crushing me. My ability to breathe and function normally has been replaced with suffocating anxiety, tears, and depression. I spend as much of my day in bed as I can. I have no reason to get up. Once all the arrangements are made I have nothing to keep my mind occupied and it's torture. Depression is a deep sorrow but anxiety is the real killer. Adrenaline and fear neatly packaged and deposited into the pit of your stomach. Your hands shake, you can't breathe and tears threaten to fall from your eyes for no reason at all it seems. It's impossible to focus on one task but at the same time it's impossible to sit and do nothing. It's debilitating. My brain's torturous analytical thoughts make me go insane.

Ryan, after weeks of seeing me in such a state, demands I see a doctor for help. They prescribe me antidepressants, anti-anxiety and sleeping pills. I take them faithfully every day to turn myself into a walking zombie who feels nothing. Ryan doesn't seem to care that I've changed, that the meds have changed me, that I feel nothing. He continues on with his degradation and destruction.

The funeral was beautiful. Everyone told me that much. I did a good job of bringing everyone together to celebrate a life cut short. Jenny was only twenty-seven. Her death tragic. I managed to pull myself together long enough to make it through the funeral but as soon as it ended I lost it. I fell apart. The gathering back at our house helped me pull myself back together again momentarily. Ryan sulked in a corner, angry that we had to have all these people over. People he didn't want in our house. "What's the point?" he'd said.

I was hugged and kissed and my back was rubbed more in that two hour gathering than in over the last four years with Ryan. People of course asked where he was and how this must be hitting him hard if he couldn't be at my side right now. If they only knew he was just irritated that they were in his house and avoiding us all.

By the time I had finished cleaning up that night Ryan had gone to bed without me. I sat in the dark living room alone and wept. Eventually I fell asleep on the couch. When I woke the next morning Ryan had already left for work. I moved from the couch to our bed and stayed the day there.

After over a month of staying in bed all day, Ryan's anger at me hit an all-time high. He dragged me out of bed roughly one afternoon and hauled my ass promptly to a therapist, Dr. Rand. He seems like a decent guy. Not that I could give a shit. I take my pills every day as prescribed to keep me from giving a shit. Ryan says if I won't get on with my life then he will make me, hence my now weekly appointments with Dr. Rand.

"Elle, you have to talk," Dr. Rand prompts.

"Why?"

"That's sort of the point of therapy," he says.

"What shall I talk about then Dr.?" I snip.

"What about your sister's death is bothering you the most?"

"The fact that she's DEAD," I say flatly.

He sighs at me and shakes his head. "You've got to work with me, Elle."

"I have no one."

"You have your husband," he reminds me. I snort in disgust. If he only knew. Sure, I have a husband, but I don't have one really. He is a stranger living in my house with me at best. A hateful stranger at that. A bell chimes indicating that our time for this week is up. I smile at Dr. Rand and stand.

"See you next week," I wave and exit his office.

I go home, pop some pills, and crawl into bed. Days I don't have therapy I stay in bed most of the day, occasionally getting up to eat something or use the bathroom. I read as many books as I can. It's the only thing that brings me any pleasure. I voraciously rip through romance novels pretending that I too could have love and a happy ending. Someone to cherish me...someone to cherish. But that dream's a slippery slope. It's an illusion and illusions never change into something real, but to stop dreaming altogether might as well be death.

On bad days I relive all of my and Jenny's greatest moments together. Each memory is as crystal clear as the pain that resonates in my chest from the loss of her. Those days I don't even hear Ryan grumbling, yelling at me or throwing things. Those days my thoughts are black and blue like my heart. I stare at the ceiling and talk to my sister. I ask her what the hell I should do. How to live without her. I ask her how to leave Ryan. Sometimes if I hold my breath and wait I can swear I hear her trying to answer me.

How do you know if you're crazy? If you look up crazy it says mentally deranged. If you then wonder what mentally deranged truly means it will tell you: mentally deranged patients are often filled with hate and animosity and will often demonstrate a series of disturbed behaviors. Generally, deranged individuals are trapped in their own state of mind.

I feel crazy some days but I don't exhibit the symptoms needed to be mentally deranged. However, Ryan, in my opinion, is hateful and trapped in his own state of mind and I find his behaviors disturbing. No one would ever believe this though. He is an upstanding citizen publicly.

PRESENT

ELLE

DAY 7

Small kisses rain all over my face and neck. I crack one eye open to find Colin grinning at me. "Morning, Babe." His arm coils around my waist while he rolls, positioning me on top of him. A tiny squeal escapes me and he laughs.

"Morning," I whisper as I dip my head to his and give him a soft kiss. He moans and tangles his fingers in my hair. I feel so carefree, alive and full of desire. I pull back a little and look into those mesmerizing hazel orbs before glancing at the clock. Eight thirty a.m.

"Do we have to train today?" I wrinkle my nose. "Because I'm feeling pretty lazy and content right now," I whine while his large palm wanders up and down my back.

"I believe your list says that today you have to say 'yes' to everything for the whole day." His eyes sparkle with mischief. I groan and roll off of him, planting my face in the pillow.

"Come on," he pushes, "it won't be that bad. I promise."

A finger jabs into my side, tickling me and I snort with laughter while curling into a tight ball. "Stop that!"

"Really, Elle. I think this 'yes day' could be pretty good."

"I guess we'll see won't we?" Sarcasm drips from my voice.

"Well then, would you like to hit the gym?" His eyes are playful and his dimple gives him a boyish charm.

"Yes," I chuckle and roll out of the warm bed to get the first shower. If I have to look at his perfectly sculpted chest and abs for another minute I might explode. As I snag a clean towel from the closet I steal one more look at him. His eyes are trained on my ass with nothing but appreciation glowing on his face. I laugh and toss the towel at him before stepping into the bathroom.

After a delicious breakfast of eggs and bacon made by Colin we hit the gym and work some more on my combinations. I'm slowly improving and toning up. My muscles ache in a good way.

"So Elle...." Colin drawls as we head out of the gym. "Care for some sushi this afternoon?"

I hate sushi. Well, I've never tried it but the idea of it totally turns me off. I wrinkle my nose at him. "I don't like sushi," I tell him.

"Would you like sushi, Elle?" His eyes glimmer.

I sigh, knowing what he's doing. "Yes." His grin widens and he extends his arm out to me.

"Well then, I know just the place." We're seated not long after arriving and as we're looking over the menu Colin seems quite pleased with himself.

"I think it's unfair to have to say yes to things I don't like," I pout.

"Well how will you experience new things if you always say no?"

"You're annoying." My pout turns to a scowl and he laughs at me. I love that laugh. It fills up a part of my heart I wasn't aware existed.

"Fine, then you order for me because I have no idea what any of this is," I say, waving my hand over the menu. When the waitress comes Colin does order for the both of us.

When our food arrives something I'm told are Avo-Kyu and California rolls are placed in front of us. They look icky. Colin picks one up. "Open up," he says as he tries to feed it to me. I clamp my mouth shut and shake my head no. "It's yes day Elle, open up." Reluctantly I open my mouth as he puts the end of the roll into my mouth and I take a bite. I chew slowly and to my surprise, it's not that bad.

"I ordered rolls with avocado in them, since I know you like those," he says with pride, recalling our grocery store evening.

"It actually wasn't so bad. I was expecting a hunk of raw fish or something," I chuckle.

Colin eats more than I do. It's all right but I'm still not totally sold, so I end up having one California roll and half an Avo-Kyu roll.

"You must be starving," he says as we're leaving. As if on cue my stomach grumbles.

"A little."

"Would you like something else?" he laughs.

"Mmmm I could go for a bagel with lots of cream cheese," I sing.

"Whatever the lady wishes," he says and smiles down at me.

Colin leads me a few blocks in the opposite direction from my cottage and into a little hole in the wall with no sign. "Best bagels in town," he declares as we step through the entrance.

"How would anyone even know this place is here?"

"You have to be a local," he says and winks. I order myself an everything bagel toasted with veggie cream cheese and dig in.

"Oh my god you're right, this is delicious," I say around a mouthful, earning me his dimpled grin.

"Do you like rides?" he asks.

"I guess. I haven't been on any in years." I shrug.

"Let's go to Carowinds."

"The amusement park?" I ask, wide-eyed.

"Yeah."

"Uh. Okay. But you'll have to drive since I'm without a car, but I'll pay for the tickets."

"No, no, this yes day is on me," he demands politely. He doesn't know I have money but I've seen his apartment, the gym. I know he gets by but isn't rolling in it and I don't want to put him out.

"Colin."

"What is it?"

"I have plenty of money. Please let me pay. Especially for things that are a direct result of the list. I'll let you have dates, but the list comes out of my pocket." I don't want to hurt his ego but some of the things on the list were only feasible because Jenny and I both had the funds to know we could do them. He looks at me in a funny way.

"Will you be my sugar mama?" he asks and laughs, knowing the only answer I can give today is yes. I roll my eyes at him. "Yes," I say, playing along.

With that we walk back to his apartment where he changes and then drives me to mine so I can do the same before leaving for Carowinds. The drive to the amusement park passes quickly as we banter back and forth with ease. When we arrive he takes my hand and laces his fingers through mine as we walk the entrance. It all feels so natural.

"Is this okay?" he asks, looking at our entwined hands.

"Yes." I smile up at him. He chuckles and the corners of his eyes crease with his smile. It's hot and makes my belly flutter.

After asking me ten times if I want to go on this ride or that, knowing all the while that I have to say yes, we've ridden almost every ride in the park and we're spent. The roller coasters left me feeling exhilarated and full of life. My cheeks hurt from smiling so much. Throughout our time wandering through the park he was sweet and attentive and I felt like I couldn't get close enough to him. Everything between us is effortless and natural.

I quite enjoyed the few times I was behind him in line, each movement forward showing his perfect butt shifting behind his jeans. His stare burns me like his touch does and he always seems to be staring. He keeps his fingers laced with mine whenever possible. His lips find my temple for no reason at all multiple times making my pulse quicken each time. We fit together in a way I didn't think possible for two people.

"Your place or mine tonight?" he asks quietly as we pull into town.

"Um. Either is fine I guess."

"Mine then," he states.

We pull into his parking spot, both exiting the car tired from a long day of fun and excitement. I'm sleepy and content as he leads me up the stairs, hand at the small of my back. As soon as we're inside and the door clicks shut behind us Colin's hands are on me. "Can I kiss you?" he breathes, pulling me hard into him. I look into those hazel eyes and lose myself.

"Yes."

His lips come to mine, taking their time exploring and worshiping. I moan into his mouth, spurring him on. His tongue finds mine and a rush of adrenaline spikes though my body making my belly clench in anticipation. He walks us slowly backward, careful to keep me upright with him as his kisses continue to rain down on me. He moves from my lips to my ear and down my neck to my collarbone. I feel a frantic desire to have more of him. I move my hands under and up his shirt, lifting it over his head and tossing it to the floor.

When my lips come to his chest his breath hitches and his muscles twitch. His fingers leave a trail of goose bumps from my hips up to my armpits as he removes my shirt. "Can I kiss you here?" he whispers hoarsely inches from my bra clad nipple.

"Yes," I breathe. His mouth comes over my breast making me whimper. "I love the noises you make," he groans before unclasping my bra and letting it drop to the floor between us. His arms scoop me up effortlessly. "I'm so desperate for you I'm afraid it's not natural," he murmurs in my ear. His hot breath cascades down my neck making me tremble as he lays me on the bed. "Can I remove these?" His fingers toy with the button of my jeans.

"Yes," I nod and he quickly rids me of my pants before doing the same. Laying there exposed in just my panties under his intense gaze makes my pulse beat erratically. I don't dare move. His eyes travel from my lips slowly and thoroughly over every inch until stopping at my ankles. When our eyes meet again his are wild with desire.

"May I touch you?" His voice is barely audible. My

throat is unable to respond so I nod at him. He moves slightly, kneeling over me. One hand coming to my neck and trailing down over my collarbone to my breast, lavishing it with attention for a moment before moving on to the other one. I gasp and my back arches up off the bed. A slight smile breaks out over his face before he licks his lips and dips his head down to me.

His kisses and nibbles following the trail of fire left behind from his fingers, his hand still slowly moving south over the flat plain of my stomach, my hip, and resting at my upper thigh. When his mouth catches up to his hands resting spot he repeats the process all the way back up my body. I feel like I'm on fire. My hips buck and a strangled sound rips from my throat. His fingers stop and brush back and forth over one of my scars. It startles me and I look down to him.

"Is this from him?" His eyes are hard and full of rage.

"Yes."

"How?" he asks through gritted teeth.

"A bowl of hot chili." His mouth kisses the scar with such tenderness that I can feel my eyes glistening with tears.

"You're gorgeous, Elle." His mouth is on mine again this time desperate with need. It's a furious kiss. Passionate and heady. I'm left gasping and panting for air when he finally pulls back. A playful grin on his face. "Do you want me, Elle?" he whispers.

"Yes."

As soon as the word is out of my mouth his hands are at my panties ripping them off. His boxers are shed and kicked away and his mouth and hands are everywhere as are mine. I can't seem to feel him enough. I want to know every inch of his body. When his fingers slide in between my legs I'm lost. His name rips from my lips as he sends me crashing towards orgasm. My body takes over, grinding into his hand needing, wanting more. When his fingers disappear I cry out in protest. He kisses me hungrily and moves himself under me. "Come with me, Elle," he croaks as I slip onto him. There are no words for the way he fills me. I sink my weight onto him reveling in the pleasure it brings.

A soft groan slips from my lips as his hands come to my waist, setting our rhythm. His hips lift and plunge as mine grind down and circle. Faster and faster until I'm trembling and can't see straight.

He flips us unexpectedly and continues to drive into me. Filling me up. Lightning explodes behind my eyes as my orgasm rips through me and I scream out his name again. He thrusts twice more before planting himself deep with a grunt and staying there, face buried in my neck. It feels so right. The weight of him on me. The pleasure he gave and took. I want to melt into him, into this moment forever.

His head lifts slightly, planting a kiss behind my ear. "Incredible," he breathes. The silence that follows is so intimate I'm taken aback. We lay tangled in each other's arms, his fingers playing with my hair, our eyes locked, silent. A thousand thoughts passing between us effortlessly. It's as if he's saturated my heart and soul. His hand trails up my spine slowly. "Roll over, baby," his voice is laced with seduction.

"I'll do anything you say...if you say it with your hands," I flirt back.

"Done," he murmurs as I roll onto my stomach and am treated to the most amazingly erotic massage in history as a soft sigh falls out of me.

PRESENT

ELLE

DAY 8

Everything Colin does is laced with affection for me and I don't know why. It confuses me and makes me elated at the same time. He's pouring coffee into a mug for me, humming softly along to the radio.

"Why me?" I ask feeling brave.

"What?" he turns to me.

"Why did you pick me? Why are you doing this with me?" I ask honestly. I can see the wheels turning in his head as he tries to answer. He sets the mug down on the counter and strides to me. Taking my hand in his he tugs me from my perch and leads me to the bathroom. Standing behind me in front of the mirror his eyes catch mine.

"Look at yourself," he says quietly in my ear. "Try to see what I see." His hand comes around from behind to my face. "You have the most beautiful face. Your eyes are intoxicating." His hand slides down the length of one arm. "Your skin is like silk," he whispers in my ear and I bite my lip to stop from shivering. His hand moves up my ribs until his palm is flat against my heart. "Your heart, your strength, your kindness amazes me, Elle. Your resilience," he murmurs low. Watching him in the mirror, his expression, and his tenderness does funny things to my belly. "Do you see what I see now?"

"I... I think so," I mumble.

"You still don't see it," he says, frustrated. Years of abuse have me convinced though that I'm not all those things, he thinks. That I'm not deserving of what he feels.

"I'm trying, Colin." Our eyes meet in the mirror and he holds my gaze as his fingers trail up and down my arms lazily.

"How do I make you feel?" he asks. My breath catches. I'm unsure how to answer. His eyes bore into mine while I search for words.

"Good. Safe. Special." I murmur.

"And when I do this?" he asks and I watch his head dip down, his lips meeting my neck, trailing feather light kisses from my shoulder to my ear, making my belly flutter. "Wanted," I breathe.

"Then until you believe what I see in you, believe what you feel from me." He twirls me around, enveloping me in his embrace. I rest my head on his chest and let out a breath as my arms circle his waist. This is crazy. I must be crazy for this to actually be happening.

As is our normal routine now, we hit the gym and I let loose all my anger and hurt on the heavy bag of sand until I can't lift my arms anymore. When I'm finished I lean against the wall and watch Colin and Ben spar in the ring. They're both powerful and quick. Impressive muscles contract and release with each jab and movement. It baffles me that all women don't hang out in boxers' gyms just for the view. I catch Colin's eye and Ben uses his distraction to clock him in the jaw, sending him down. Watching his head snap back makes me cringe.

"Thanks, Elle!" Ben laughs out while helping Colin to his feet. I sheepishly throw Colin an apologetic look but he just grins at me. "You'd be distracted too if your hot girl-friend was looking at you like mine was," Colin teases Ben, making me blush. Ben just laughs at him. Colin crawls out of the ring and closes the gap between us.

"Are you hurt?" I ask, gently touching his jaw.

"Naw. It's part of sparring. No worries." He leans in, giving me a chaste kiss that elicits hoots and hollers from guys working out. My face must be bright red by now but Colin seems unaffected by their cheers.

"Let me change and we can head out, yeah?" he asks.

"Sounds good."

"Why'd you say girlfriend?" I ask as we enter the bar. Ben and John are joining us at a karaoke bar uptown for the evening. All three men have agreed to sing a song and are presently attempting to get as drunk as possible in order to make that happen.

"Does it bother you?" he counters.

"I'm not sure." I snip.

"When you know, clue me in. Until then, that's what I'm calling you." His words jolt me. How is he so sure of everything?

The men have made it clear that I have to sing first or they won't at all. A show of good faith, John had laughed. Colin knows it's on the list and that I'll do it simply because I want to accomplish every last thing Jenny and I had thought up. I take a shot of something Ben brought over to settle my nerves. It burns on its way down but I choke back my cough. I don't like being the center of attention. I don't like all eyes on me and in a few moments I will be. Colin sits close while sipping his beer and rubbing soothing circles on my back. I picked "Low Road" by Grace Potter. I know the song well and it's not too high for me to sing. My knees bounce nervously as the woman on stage finishes her song.

"You can do it," I tell her after her name is called. Her bottom lip trembles and she looks nervous as hell but I can see the resolve in her eyes. This list is important to her.

When she grasps the mic and starts singing my jaw drops. She's got a gritty soulful voice that works well with the song. Her voice grows steadier with each line she sings. You can almost see her confidence pick up. Her eyes lock on mine and as she starts the second verse it's as if she's singing directly to me.

"I held on so dearly
To the wrong things in my life
But now I see so clearly
I was walking into my own knife
You've got to get up off that street
Stop looking at your feet
And take a hold of something real
And this old man, took my hand
He looked at me and said, little girl, I understand
That it's a low, low road

You've gotta roll down
Before you find your way, my friend
And it's a high, high hill
You've gotta climb up
Before you get to the top again"

Right then I know she heard me this morning in the bathroom. That she believes me. That I'm making a difference in her life. My chest grows tight listening as her voice is wrought with emotion and she finishes the song. She's stunning.

I think, from what she's told me about her sister that tonight, she'd be proud. The crowd cheers. Mostly because she didn't suck, but it brings a shy smile to her face. As she makes her way back to the table I can't tear my eyes from hers. I stand when she's within reach and pick her up, swinging her around in circles, making her giggle. Her smile is dazzling, lighting up her striking face. My stomach flutters with something for her. Pride, maybe, love even.

I set her down as Ben's name is called. We sit as he stands, swaying slightly and moves to the stage to sing "Sweet Home Alabama." He's terrible. It's the most hilarious thing ever. He's all but booed off the stage but his smile never falters. "That was awesome, right?!" he shouts at us over the buzz of the bar. We all laugh at him for having no fear of rejection. John goes next and is surprisingly good. Although, "House of the Rising Sun" isn't too hard to sing. Next up is me. I'm a little nervous but I've performed before. Not that Elle is aware of that little fact. I choose to just play the piano on the stage and skip the karaoke music.

"This is 'I Will Possess Your Heart' by Death Cab for Cutie," I say and adjust the mic at the piano. I turn slightly to find Elle's eyes. Keeping them trained on her I start moving my fingers across the keys, watching her eyes grow wide at the surprise.

> "How I wish you could see the potential,
> the potential of you and me.
> It's like a book elegantly bound but,
> in a language that you can't read.
> Just yet.
> You gotta spend some time, Love.
> You gotta spend some time with me.
> And I know that you'll find, love
> I will possess your heart.
> You gotta spend some time, Love.
> You gotta spend some time with me.
> And I know that you'll find, love
> I will possess your heart"

As I sing her eyes glimmer with tears threatening to spill over, but she's smiling and not once does her gaze waiver from mine. I sing to her and no one else. When I finish she stands and among the clapping and cheering I see her rush the stage. I hop down just before she reaches me and catch her as she jumps into my arms babbling into my ear about how amazing I am while entwining her arms and legs around me. When she pulls back to look at me I'm truly astonished. Her brilliant green eyes are burning with emotion for me. "That was the most romantic thing that's ever been done for me," she breathes in awe. "You're the most romantic thing," she says as her lips crash into mine and kisses me senseless. The little gasping noises she makes as we kiss make me harder than I already am and I want nothing more than to get her home and have my way with her.

PRESENT

DAY 9

Can you even believe that he sang for me?! I know, I know, amazing. So incredible. My heart has grown wings and flown straight into his. I'm a goner, Jenny. I can't ever go back after having a piece of him.

Last night was amazing. The four of us had so much fun. I'm still reeling over the fact that he plays piano and sings. We got home late after too many beers and too much laughing and crashed into my bed. The rain trickles in streams down my bedroom window quietly. I'm lazily draped across Colin's warm body. His face is chiseled and so handsome when he sleeps. Peaceful and innocent-looking. I can't help myself as I trail a finger lightly over each eyebrow, memorizing every detail of his face.

His eyes flutter open leisurely exposing the deep hazel color that captivates me. I don't think I could ever get sick of him, of his eyes. Of what they express wordlessly each time they meet mine. These are the moments that I wish I could get lost in them for days. Just forget the entire world and live in his gaze.

"Morning, Babe," he sighs. I kiss his chest in response before resting my head on it.

"I still can't believe you can play an instrument and sing," I gush softly.

"Still stuck on that?" he chuckles.

"Well it is pretty amazing, you know." He squeezes me gently into his lean firm frame. Every touch undoes me a little more.

"Hey," he murmurs into my hair.

"Mmm?"

"It's raining." He whispers.

"I noticed."

"It's on the list. We should take advantage of the rainy day. We don't have to go in order right?" he playfully asks.

"It's not in any order specifically…" I trail off, smirking. "I'd at least like to brush my teeth and have coffee first."

"Deal," he says, kissing my temple before rolling out of bed and disappearing into the bathroom.

I hop out of bed, stretch, and stroll to the kitchen to start the coffee maker before heading back to the bathroom. Colin smacks my butt as we pass each other, making me laugh. As I brush my teeth I can't help but wonder when all this will come crashing down around me. I have no idea if that guy Ryan hired is still looking for me or if Ryan is looking for me. I've been careful to use only cash for everything and my prepaid cell phone has only been used to call my lawyer and Colin. Still, if I'm found it would be torture waiting for everything with my lawyer to be set in motion. To be torn away from Colin and all the happiness I've found. I push the thoughts down until I don't feel them anymore, spit and rinse.

"Coffee, Dear," Colin says. He has the worst fake English accent ever.

"Brilliant!" I give it a try, sounding equally lame. We both fall into a fit of laughter. We sit tucked into each other on the couch, me reading a book, Colin flipping through the paper, enjoying our coffee.

"Elle?" Something is off. I can hear it in his tone. I shut the book, giving him my full attention.

"What is it?" I question.

He folds the section of the paper in half then hands it to me. My picture, albeit a blonde me, stares back at me.

"South Carolina husband pleads for return of wife who went missing over a week ago

A South Carolina husband is pleading for the return of his wife after she vanished without a trace over a week ago. At a candlelight vigil held outside their home Saturday night, Ryan Darling spoke out publicly for this first time since Elle Darling disappeared, the Daily Herald reported.

'Elle, if you can see this, I want you home. I love you. I miss you,' Darling, who was the first to report her missing, said. It's possible that Darling's missing wife may be a danger to herself. If seen, please contact the local police."

My coffee drops to the ground, spilling everywhere and startling me. I immediately drop the paper, scrambling to the kitchen for paper towels to clean the mess. I'm trembling violently upon return, dropping to my knees, trying to sop up the mess I've made. Unexpectedly I'm hoisted off the floor, turned and seated on Colin's lap. His hands come to either side of my face, forcing me to look at him.

"It's okay. I won't let you go back," he says in a hushed voice. "I won't let you go back to that," he says determinedly. His face is strong and firm. I nod once before my head tumbles to his chest and the tears start.

"Elle," he says softly after a moment. "Why does it say you're a possible danger to yourself?" I sniffle, trying to kill a second.

"I...it's probably just a ploy he's using," I lie. The second the lie is out of my mouth I feel despicable. He continues to rub my back tenderly while guilt washes over me. Why I can't tell him everything, I don't know. I just can't. It might change the way he looks at me and I couldn't bear that. I'm finally in control, and comfortable with who I am right now. I don't want to relive or rehash that day.

"I'm sorry about the mess," I grouse.

"Elle, who cares about spilled coffee?" He asks looking horrified at my reaction.

"Ryan. Ryan would have. He would have screamed and thrown things and expected me to tend to it immediately." Embarrassment and shame cover my face. He lifts my chin until I'm eye to eye with him.

"I'm. Not. Him," he says firmly.

"I know! I know, Colin. It's been years though. I can't undo years in a week. I'm trying. Really. I am." His eyes take in mine and he kisses me sweetly.

Standing abruptly, he carries me out the back door onto the deck. The rain is pelting down now, the water saturating us almost instantly. He sets me to my feet carefully and watches me silently. I can feel my hair matted to the sides of my face, dripping at the ends. Each drop hitting the tops of my breasts. My breathing erratic. Rivulets of water make unpredictable paths down Colin's face, darting this way and that. I have to blink rapidly to keep the water out of my eyes as I look up to his face. A streamlet of water cascades down his handsome face pooling at his chin before dripping off. I push up on my toes and catch it with my tongue. He's rooted to his spot simply watching my every move. His shirt clings to him, making me want to mold my soft spots with his hard. When a droplet of rain drips from the end of his nose onto his upper lip I wrap my arms around his neck while on my tip toes and pull him to me. My tongue darts out, capturing the bead of water as I slowly run my tongue over his soft warm lips.

He comes unglued from his spot then. Hands fisting my hair and pulling me impossibly further into him. His kiss is hard, deep, and frantic as we desperately try to cling to each other. One hand trails the length of my spine to the top of my ass, pushing me into his hardness. I moan against his teeth, gasping for air as a shot of heat lands straight between my legs.

He moves his lips to my neck, licking and sucking the tributaries from me. I push against him, sending us tumbling back into the house, me landing on top of him, a puddle gathering under us. We fight to strip off our wet clothes without breaking contact. Shucking everything away, he rolls me under him and plunges in. Pulling out and pushing in, my hips buck wildly, needing more. "Come with me, Elle," he says and thrusts over and over, deeper and deeper, making every nerve in my body stand at attention until my legs quiver uncontrollably and I come hard with him. We lay in a wet mess on the living room floor panting for air, tangled in each other's arms.

"I think we covered kissing in the rain pretty well," I say, my voice breathy and uneven.

"I think you're right," he chuckles, then sobers, his eyes glimmering with truth. "I'm never letting you go, Elle." The sincerity and warmth emulating from him sucks the air from my lungs and I'm sure my eyes bug out. "I don't want you to," I admit. We lay knotted together on the hard floor just being.

PRESENT

ELLE

DAY 10

"Faster, Elle. Jab, cross, hook. Move your feet," Colin pushes. We're in the ring sparring together. He's quick and skilled and my attempts barely make contact. Sweat drips down my chest and back. My breath comes in short bursts as I try to land a good one on him. Someone walks by the ring and in Colin's moment of distraction I implement his teachings, catching him with a hook and sending him stumbling backwards a few steps. The moment it happens my arms fall to my sides and panic sweeps through me as I rush to his side.

"I'm so sorry! Are you all right?" I pant at him. He shakes it off, smiling at me.

"That was great! You're getting much better," he encourages. A slow smile spreads over my face and warms my belly.

"Yeah?"

"Yeah. Now come on, let's go again." And then we're back at it. I've been learning how to block, dodge, and keep control of myself until I can land a winning shot. It's a great workout but Colin's also doing this for a reason outside the list now, so I can protect myself if needed or at least put up a fight. Our second time around I land a couple of good jabs but mostly dart around the ring blocking. I know Colin goes easy on me with the force of his hits but he doesn't go easy in any other way and ends up kicking my butt. I'm spent and in desperate need of a shower.

"Go shower. You did great today," he affirms.

"You still kicked my ass," I jest.

"You're still seven inches shorter and ninety pounds lighter. You did good," he says firmly as if he's willing me to believe it, in myself. I climb between the ropes, hopping down to the mats and head for my much needed shower.

"So I'll see you at one?" I ask, freshly showered.

"Yeah, I'll pick you up," Colin replies before leaning in and stealing a kiss and my breath.

The sun beats down on me as I make the short walk to my cottage. *Jenny, I'm missing you like crazy today. I wish you could know Colin. I wish you could see my smile. The way he treats me.* I blow out a breath and smile up to the clouds as if she can see me.

I walk around the cottage and follow the path to the beach. The wind whips my hair around my face as I sink into the sand and lean back. I close my eyes, listening to the waves crashing at the shore and letting the sun warm me. I have a feeling it's going to be a good day.

"Elle?" A deep voice carries over the wind. "Elle!" My eyes drift open and I'm briefly confused as I take in my surroundings. Pushing up onto my elbows I realize I've fallen asleep on the beach. "Elle!!" Colin's voice carries with the wind, now worried and frantic.

"Down here!" I shout towards the cottage. His large frame appears at the crest of the dune, his face troubled until he sees me.

"Crap. You scared me. You weren't at home and didn't answer your cell," he says, plopping down next to me and brushing a wild strand of hair out of my face.

"Sorry," I yawn. "I fell asleep out here."

"Late night?" he winks.

"One could say that," I flirt back.

"Tommy's expecting us at the shelter in half an hour."

"Well then, let's go!" I brush the sand off my hands and take Colin's outreached hand, letting him pull me up. His fingers tangle in my hair and he tousles it around playfully.

"Sand," he explains when I duck and squeal at him. I grab his hand, twining our fingers together and tug him towards the path, chuckling. Ben's friend Tommy runs an animal shelter just outside of town and happily agreed to let Colin and I volunteer for the afternoon. I adore animals. We always had dogs or cats growing up. Ryan detests pets and would never allow us one so I'm excited to spend the afternoon showering attention on the abandoned animals at the shelter.

Because of my unexpected nap on the beach we're a smidge late arriving at the Fontaine Animal Shelter. A tall thin man approaches us with a warm smile in the lobby.

"Colin! Good to see you again," he says.

"You too, Tommy. Thanks for having us today," Colin says and takes his hand, shaking it firmly.

"This is Elle. Elle, this is Tommy, the man in charge."

"Nice to meet you, Tommy."

"Likewise." He claps his hands together, smiling. "Shall I put you two to work?"

Colin and I nod our heads and follow Tommy's lead through a set of double doors. Rows and rows of cages line a long hallway. Dogs of all shapes, sizes, and ages bark and wag their tails at our approach.

"We have fifty dogs right now and we're perpetually short staffed. Generally we have the volunteers feed, bathe, and walk them. They've already been fed this morning though so you can skip that." He shows Colin and I to the bathing station and where the supplies are before showing us where to find the leashes. Once we're comfortable with what we've been tasked with Tommy leaves us, returning to his office.

"Well... let's get started," I prompt. Colin and I fall effortlessly into an easy routine. I bring the dogs one at a time while he washes them. I dry and bring them back. Colin is drenched after the first five dogs, making us both roll with laughter every time another one shakes, sending water flying. At four we stop washing, letting Tommy know which dog we stopped at. I grab two leashes and pick the two most pathetic-looking dogs to start with. I couldn't resist their big sad eyes and wagging tails.

"I think more water hit you than the dogs," I giggle to Colin as we walk around the block.

"It feels that way," he chuckles, glancing down at his water-logged shirt and back to me.

"You should have washed." He waggles his brows at me and stares at my white tee shirt.

"Perv," I say and smack him playfully on the arm.

"Yup." He grins.

We manage to walk eight dogs by the time the shelter is closing. The five hours spent together today were wonderful. There's something about giving selflessly that makes me feel good about myself. Colin was a champ too, never complaining and more than happy to be at my side. It's easy being with him, almost too easy. A tiny part of my brain is still waiting for his true colors to come flying out when I least expect it. My gut, though, tells me that I've found something rare and shouldn't hold back. I can't ignore the inexplicable draw I feel to him so I shove all my doubt away as best I can.

"Thank you two so much, you were a great help today," Tommy gushes as he walks us to Colin's car.

"Could we come back again sometime? I really enjoyed today."

"Elle, you can come back anytime you want. Give me a ring anytime." He smiles warmly at me. I follow Colin's lead, folding into the car and waving my goodbye as we pull out of the parking lot.

"I had so much fun. Who knew!?" Colin's velvet smooth laugh fills the car.

"Thank you," I say.

"For what?"

"For being you. For doing these things with me. For wanting to do these things with me."

He stops at the intersection and looks to me. "I think you'd find I'd do anything for you." His gaze is smoldering. "Let's go home. Want to order out tonight?" And that's when I know that home is together. That he's just as satisfied with me as I am with him. Warmth seeps through my chest and my heart swells at the thought. The light turns green and we continue on towards my cottage, fingers tangled together and woozy with the full feeling in my heart.

PAST

2011

I stop and look in the mirror in the waiting room. I hardly recognize myself. My hair is lifeless and dull. My eyes have dark circles around them and there's no light in them anymore. They look dead. My clothes hang off me. I must have lost a lot of weight, not that I had a lot to lose to begin with at five foot five and a hundred thirty pounds. I look old, frail, and weathered now.

"Tell me something about yourself, Elle," Dr. Rand prods.

"Like what?"

"Well, since you don't want to talk about your sister maybe we should start with you."

"I like to read."

"Oh? Fiction? Non-fiction?" he pushes.

"Fiction mostly... romance novels."

"Ahh. I see."

"What do you see?" I ask.

"Do you read to escape?"

I shrug my shoulders. "My marriage isn't the greatest," I state.

"Explain that statement further."

"Ryan treats me like shit. Is that clear enough?" I clip.

"Elle, I'm here to listen, not judge."

"Well he does. Jenny was trying to help me leave him. He's..." I trail off, unsure of how to approach this. Ryan found Dr. Rand and meets with him monthly to check on my progress. I think it's strange.

"You're leaving your husband?" he questions, scribbling notes on his pad.

"No. I wanted to. I want to. But, with Jenny gone.... I don't know. I don't know how."

"Have you talked to Ryan about this? Tried counseling?"

"Ryan believes counseling is for pussies. So he says. I've tried changing. I've tried talking. I've tried getting him to talk. I've tried taking all the blame. I've tried giving all the blame. I've tried anger and arguing and doing whatever I can to make him happy. None of it affects him. None of it changes anything."

"Interesting," he mumbles. The scratching of his pencil on the paper in his lap grates on my nerves and makes my anxiety spike.

"You can't tell him any of this, correct?" My knee bounces nervously.

"Right."

"So, at your progress meetings, how do you inform him of any updates on me? What is he paying you?" I ask.

"Elle, your husband loves you. He is worried about your state of mind since Jenny's death and he simply asks that I keep him in the loop regarding your mental health."

"That's not an answer." The bell chimes, letting us know that our time is up. I'm irritated that Dr. Rand ignores my last statement and sends me on my way. It makes the hair on the back of my neck stand up. It makes me not trust him. What is the point of therapy if you don't trust your therapist?

As always, I go home and crawl into bed. *Jenny, what the hell am I doing? How do I get out of this? I need you. I miss you. I don't want to be a wreck. I don't want to be sad. I want to leave my awful marriage and start a new happy life alone.* I wanted to do it with my sister at my side but that option has been taken from me. Yet still, she'd want me to get the hell out of dodge even if she wasn't with me.

When my parents passed away they left me their house and money. A nice big house in a nice part of town. I grew up in this house. I loved this house until Ryan moved in. Now I hate this house. I hate all the hate that lives in the house. Ryan will never divorce or leave me. It would leave him dependent on his salary alone and homeless. His salary should be enough but he blows through it at an alarming rate. He needs my money to sustain his lifestyle. He thinks I don't know this, but I'm not stupid.

With Jenny gone, I've inherited not only my half of our parents estate but hers too plus her estate. I don't need to work. I keep it all very separate from Ryan because he is a financial disaster and has come close to bankrupting us numerous times over the years. His backup plan is me and my "bailout account," as he calls it. I've always worked so that my salary is what I have to pay bills and spend with. I don't like touching any of the inheritance money and Jenny would certainly not want any of her cash touching Ryan's hands.

I hear the door slam closed at six on the nose and heavy

footsteps walking around downstairs. I can tell simply from the sound of his stomping that he's not happy. The house is a mess. All his mess, since I keep to the bedroom these days. Dinner isn't on the table and won't be, and I'm in bed, yet again. He didn't come home last night. I was thankful at the time but it probably means he was out gambling away more money. As his steps draw near our bedroom door my heart rate spikes and my palms get clammy in anticipation.

"What the fuck, Elle!" are the first words out of his mouth when he comes barreling through the door. I stare at him blankly, waiting. "You've got to snap out of this. It's been months! You look like shit... you won't put out... I'm STARVING... the house is disgusting and you still don't have a goddamned job yet!" he finishes. All I can think of while staring at him is that he is the most selfish person I've ever met.

"Ryan, this isn't about you... it's about me. I'll cope and move on and get past this on my terms and schedule," I tell him, struggling to keep my voice steady.

"Like hell you will! Oh, sure, it's about you... what about how it's affecting ME though?"

"I don't care how it affects you. I'm only worried about me right now," I say as calmly as possible.

"FUCK YOU ELLE! Are you even capable of doing anything right? You sit here in this room all alone day after day." He storms over to where I sit on the bed and grabs me by the shoulders roughly. "ENOUGH!" he screams while shaking me hard like a rag doll. He's never been physical with me like this and it leaves me stunned and trembling. The rage emanating from his eyes is terrifying. I stare up at him with vacant eyes unable to comprehend that this morning when I woke my life was shit but now in the span of ten hours it's infinitely worse. Everything has changed.

He stops shaking me suddenly, his eyes furiously searching mine for something, anything. When he finds nothing but my blank stare he swings his arm back and slaps me hard across the face. "Do you even feel anything?" he screeches as my head snaps left. I begin to right myself when his hand comes again knocking me sideways. My hand flies to my cheek. It stings and I taste blood where his wedding ring caught my lip, how ironic. My heart stopped beating, my lungs felt like they collapsed and my skin was suddenly too tight over my body.

Determination pulses through me. In a rush I push him away and stand on shaking legs. "This is the last time you tell me I've got it wrong. The last time I let you in." My voice breaks slightly but I won't let him see me cry over him. I brush past him, exiting our bedroom and darting down the stairs.

"Dammit, Elle. I'm sorry!" he shouts after me. I don't stop. I snag my keys off the counter on my way out the door. I get in my car, throw it in reverse, and peel out the driveway.

I've lied to people for him. I've covered for him all this time. Downplaying all the terrible words he's said to me, things he's destroyed, and for what? Did I think my lies would come true? That he was kind and caring? That he didn't mean what he did? There's a moment of truth in my lies and tears fall down my face at an alarming rate but I don't feel sad. My thoughts are crystal clear. I've never felt so perfectly in tune with myself before.

I speed down our road not giving a shit about Ryan or that my life has shattered and splintered right in front of my eyes. The tree at the bend in the road is thick and old and gnarly. Deeply rooted in its spot. I punch the gas pedal to the floor and close my eyes. In a moment I will be free. I will have my sister and my parents back and I will be me again. The sound of crunching metal assaults my ears. The impact jars my body. I taste blood. Pain rockets through me. Then, everything goes black. This is it.

PRESENT

ELLE

DAY 11

*"Went to The Freaky Bean to pick up a book.
Coffee and pastries to come. Stay tuned...
xx
Elle"*

I leave Colin sleeping in bed and head to the cafe from last week. I want to get the book from the lovely Jenna. I could have easily downloaded it to my Kindle but part of me wants to keep the connection with her, so off I go. When I arrive she's already claimed a table out front and is sitting quietly reading and sipping her coffee.

"Hi."

"You came!" Jenna elates.

"I did. I'm hoping I could take you up on the offer to borrow the book if you've finished."

She leans down, digging through the bag at her feet and pops back up furnishing the book we'd talked about.

"I brought it just in case you showed today." Her smile is bright and intoxicating. I find myself grinning broadly just from the sight of it.

"Thank you so much. I really appreciate it. When I finish, will I find you here to return it?" I ask.

"Every Friday morning, Honey." We carry on for a few more moments before I enter the café, ordering coffees and treats for Colin and I. By the time I'm back home Colin is up, sitting on the deck reading the paper. I almost hate to interrupt. It's a treat watching him without him knowing. The way he runs his hand through his hair each time he flips a page makes my chest tight. When he crosses and uncrosses his legs the muscles twitch and bulge. He's really a sight to see. He's beautiful. Something catches his attention and his head slowly turns his hazel eyes, meeting mine with a smile.

"You're back! Where are these pastries you speak of?" he jokes. I sit down next to him, set our coffees down, and pull out the treats.

"A raspberry cheese Danish, two cinnamon rolls, and one of those little blueberry tart things," I say triumphantly.

"That's a lot of pastries for two people." His lips twitch at the corners.

"Well ... I kinda wanted a little of all of them and I couldn't decide.... so.... I went with gluttony over practicality." I shrug. He laughs loud and hard and it makes my heart beat wildly. I love hearing it. I love his smile. His mouth. He picks up the Danish and eyes me mischievously. "Open up, Ellie," he badgers. I do as I'm told and open for a bite. He slides the Danish into my mouth and as I start to bite down he smashes it all over my face. I squeal and stare at him wide-eyed before bursting out laughing.

"You just ruined a perfectly delicious Danish!" I squawk at him.

"Man," he laughs, "note to self: don't mess with Elle's pastries."

I scrape a giant hunk off my chin and smush it across his lips. He licks them and moans.

"Oh man, that is seriously one amazing Danish." He moans.

"Now you understand," I laugh at him. I wipe my face off and we finish our treats without wasting anymore.

"There's a Rock Gym two towns over," he informs me. "We can head over anytime."

"Nice." I answer.

"Why rock climb?" he asks.

"I don't know, it was just something neither one of us had ever done. We, ah, weren't very outdoorsy. I guess it was to try something outside our normal comfort zone. Plus Jenny was afraid of heights so it would have been kinda monumental for her."

"Well then, we do this for Jenny." He raises his coffee cup in a toast.

"For Jenny," I parrot and clink my cup to his.

Her fingers glide through her hair as she pulls it up and knots it loosely at the top of her head. A guide is strapping her into a harness and the way the straps cut across each half globe of her rear makes my dick twitch. Her yoga pants hug every inch of her in the most alluring way. I watch as her tank rides up exposing the skin at her waist for a moment before her graceful fingers tug it back into place. Her face lights up at something the guide says and a pang of jealousy hits me. She's the most beautiful creature. I don't particularly care for other men witnessing her stunning smile. It's selfish but I want those smiles she gives for myself. He tugs the rope, checking it before telling us that we're all set. Her green eyes capture mine, gleaming with excitement.

"Ready?" I ask and her head bounces her nod yes.

She reaches up and grabs hold of the first craggy hand-hold, propelling herself upwards, the sinew of her arms holding her as she finds her footing. She's hesitant and slow the first few feet but soon works herself into a comfortable pattern. Hand, footing, hand, pull. I keep her pace left of her.

"Colin, I can't find a footing." She glances down the twenty feet that we've climbed and looks a little squeamish.

"Don't look down now, we only have five more feet to the top. Can you move your left foot up and to the left? There's a footing there you should be able to reach."

I watch as she tries to move in the direction I've told her but her leg falls just short of reaching.

"I can't reach," she huffs.

"Move your hands left. You can hold on while you push off the right footing to catch the left one."

"It's too far."

"It's not."

"It is."

"Elle."

"You're annoying," she grumbles. She angles her body at a slant and swings her body left. Her foot lands just where it should then slips. Fear flashes in her eyes and she scrambles to right herself. When she finally does I hear her blow out a breath.

"Fine, you were right," she admits. We finish the climb

together. Twenty-five feet up to the top and she made it. I let her ring the bell at the top.

"Now for the fun part," I chuckle as we both lean back into our sit bones and start to rappel down the wall. By the time we reach the bottom she's wearing a triumphant face-splitting grin that makes me swell with pride for her. She's so damned adorable. I brush a loose piece of hair from her face before pulling her into my chest. I love the way it feels when her arms wrap around me. I've never felt anything so comforting.

Exhilaration filled me as we rappelled down the wall. I did it. I climbed twenty-five feet up and rang that stupid bell for Jenny. It was a fun experience but I don't anticipate becoming an avid rock climber any time soon. Colin beamed with pride as he gazed at me the entire climb. His encouragement puts me at ease. At the bottom of the wall when Colin's arms wrapped around me something unspoken passed between us. I can't figure it out. I can't identify it but it scares me a little. Things have moved too quickly. I'm too dependent on him I think. I'm supposed to be alone.

"Colin," I stare out the car window. "I think maybe things are moving too fast."

"Are you talking about us?" He sounds genuinely shocked at my words.

"Yes." My voice shakes.

"Why?" His voice croaks.

"We've only known each other a week... we've, well, you know, moved quickly."

"That's true but it doesn't feel wrong to me."

"It doesn't feel wrong to me either but that's what scares me. That it's too effortless. That it's not sustainable. That the other shoe will drop and when it does you'll be hurt." I ramble.

"Why me?" He asks gently.

"Because. Because I'm married. Because even though I've been estranged from him for almost a year, he still scares me. I'm supposed to be finding me, not losing myself to another relationship."

"Dammit, Elle." His eyes are dark and his jaws clenched.

"I'm sorry, Colin. I just don't think it's safe to be together, or healthy. It's all too fast." I know what I'm saying is wrong, Colin is right for me but my fears are valid too. I can't let anything hurt him.

"We can slow down," he pleads gently.

"I don't know." I shake my head.

"Elle. I don't care what you say. I'm not giving you up. I don't care how fast and impossible it feels, it's happening and it's incredible. You're incredible." His words are touching and my resolve crumbles slightly.

"I need to think about it. I'll still train tomorrow morning." I offer.

"I hate what he's done to you," he grits through his teeth.

"What are you talking about?"

"He's stripped you of the ability to think you deserve love. To accept it. You're fearful of it. He's made you lose the part of yourself that believes in you, that lets you trust your own gut." Tears threaten to fall at his words. He's right. I know he's right but it doesn't change how real my pathetic feelings feel or that I feel them at all. So I don't say anything more.

The remainder of our ride is spent in silence, me staring out the window, lost in the lush green scenery flying past and him white knuckling the steering wheel. When he drops me off at the cottage I quickly dart inside, collapsing on my bed before the first sob escapes me. *What have I done, Jenny? Why does this hurt? Why aren't you fucking answering me?!*

After hours of sobbing and overanalyzing every last detail of our time together I realize that maybe I'd just found what I'd been hoping for all these years. Maybe, although fast, Colin and I are a good thing. I am more my own person now than I was a year, even three years ago. So much has changed in so little time and I've changed, grown. I know what I want in life now. I've taken steps to make it happen...illegal steps, but what's the difference? I fight for me and what I want now, I don't lay down and take anything and my heart wants Colin. I hide in my room, wallowing in the self-pity that seems to be drowning me. I cry some more, wondering if I've gone and messed up possibly the most amazing thing to ever happen to me before falling into a fitful sleep.

PAST

My eyes slowly fluttered open as a multitude of alarms, whistles, buzzes, an ice machine disgorging its cubes, a laundry cart rolling, an IV pump beeping, and voices discussing good and bad outcomes rape my senses. It's too bright. I slam my eyes shut again taking in all the foreign sounds. This doesn't sound like I imagined. I don't know if I truly thought there was a Heaven or a Hell but wherever I was supposed to end up, this is not it.

"Elle....Elle can you hear me?" The voice sounds distant yet too close. I pry my eyes open once more and squint at the figure hovering above me. "Where am I?" I rasp. My throat is impossibly dry and my voice doesn't sound like it belongs to me. Someone touches my wrist and pain rockets through me at the slight movement, making me whimper.

"Just getting your vitals," a different voice mumbles.

"Elle, I'm Dr. Evers. You're at St. Francis Hospital. Do you remember anything?"

"Car accident," I scratch.

"Yes. Good, you remember. You were in a car accident. Your left arm, collarbone, and left leg are badly broken. I'm going to give you something for the pain. It will make you drowsy though," the doctor says. I still can't quite see clearly to really make him out. I try to nod my head but pain rips through me when I try. "Don't try to move. Just relax and rest," he says.

"Water," I grate.

"Yes, the nurse can bring you water." Moments later a blurry figure sits next to me and a straw comes to my lips. I pull lightly on the straw, drawing water into my mouth. It's cool and refreshing, instantly making me feel slightly better.

"What day is it?" I quietly ask.

"January tenth," the doctor's voice replies. That can't be right. It's the sixth. I know it's the sixth. As if sensing my confusion he continues, "You've been in a coma for four days, Elle. We're glad to see you finally awake." He squeezes my right hand lightly before leaving the room. Four days? I've been here for four days?!

My vision is slowly improving. I glance around the room. There are three flower arrangements on various tables and a few cards propped up surrounding them. The nurse with the water is at the end of the bed writing on a whiteboard. "Who are those from?" I ask, eyeing the flowers. She turns and reads off a few names of good friends that I haven't seen for a while. None of them are from my husband. "Has anyone visited?" I push her further.

"Your husband has visited two nights for a little while." Her eyes look sad. Pity sad. Whose husband visits twice in four days? Mine does. "Thanks," I say, avoiding her eyes. Another nurse enters and hooks something up to my IV and moments later I drift to sleep.

When I open my eyes again I find him at my door. He's wearing his best apology but I remember. I took what he dished out. There are no words to hide behind now. Just me and him alone and I won't let him hurt me anymore.

"Elle," he breathes.

"Get out," I clip through gritted teeth.

"Calm down. We need to talk," he pushes.

"We have nothing to talk about. Get out." Machines start beeping frantically around me.

"Excuse me, sir." The nurse I talked to the day before brushes past him to the heart rate monitor beeping wildly. "Sir, she needs to stay calm."

"I need him to leave," I tell the nurse, my eyes frenzied. She looks between us for a moment then nods her head.

"I need to ask you to leave, sir."

"I'm her goddamned husband for Christ's sake!" he bellows.

"I'm sorry, sir, but it's imperative that we keep her relaxed and calm right now." She moves a step towards Ryan in challenge.

"You can't keep me out forever, Elle, we have things to discuss concerning your... stay," he relents, turning on his heel and leaving the room. If I can, I will keep him out forever. I can't imagine how I'm going to do that but there has to be a way.

"Thank you," I sigh to the nurse. "What's your name?"

"Rachel."

"Hi Rachel. Elle. Nice to actually meet you." I try to be charming.

"It's nice to finally hear your voice. It was touch and go there for a while. Just glad you woke up." She smiles. She has a nice smile, too. It's big and bright and reaches her eyes.

"Can I ask you something?"

"Shoot," she answers.

"How long before I get out of here?" I ask, knowing I have a while but it would be nice to have some sort of time frame for sanity's sake. Her smile falls just slightly. "I mean, I know I'm pretty beat up, but I just want a ballpark," I try to joke.

"Honey," she starts. "It's not just the injuries you've sustained. You're on suicide watch. This is the Psych floor." Her words leave me speechless and dazed. A tear slips out the corner of one eye and trickles down my face slowly before hitting my lip. I lick it away, tasting the salty wetness and let my head drop back on the pillow.

"You weren't just in an accident, you caused the accident," she continues. I don't need her to tell me though, I was there. I knew what I was doing. I knew what was supposed to happen and just like Ryan always alludes, I failed at it. I am so pathetic that I couldn't even succeed at ending my own life. I clear my throat. "I'm aware, thanks."

I hear her move towards the door. "Wait!" I call after her. "I would really prefer to have no visitors if that's possible, not even my husband," I advise her. She nods her head twice and leaves.

PAST

2012
February

My feelings suffocate me. I struggle to come to terms with the fact that I'm in the Psych ward on suicide watch. What can I do, though? I can't walk. I only have one good arm and one good leg right now and a broken collarbone to boot. How much of a threat do they think I really pose to myself in this state? The doctor explains that once my injuries heal there will be significant physical therapy needed to get me back to good. Until then I will be meeting with Dr. Rand twice a week. He has graciously informed the hospital what drugs I was taking and those too will now be added to my daily regimen.

"Elle. Good to see you," Dr. Rand quips as he sits by my bed.

"Hi," I reply flatly.

"We've got a lot to cover this week dontcha think?" Is he trying to piss me off?

"Sure." I roll my head left and stare out the barred window.

"I want you to take a look at these," he says. I swing my head back toward him. He's holding a few pictures out to me. I reach out, grabbing them and look them over.

"What do you see?" he probes.

"I see my car. Mangled." The pictures are of the accident. Judging by the car and tree, how I survived is a mystery.

"And... how does that make you feel?"

"Like a failure," I tell him honestly.

"Come again?" One eyebrow is cocked and his nose is curled up on one side, making him look ridiculous.

"It makes me feel like a failure. The car is clearly obliterated yet I am not. I attempted to kill myself yet here I am. A survivor of that wreckage." I toss the photos back at him.

He sits motionless for a moment. "I see. Do you still want to die?"

"What kind of question is that? No I don't want to die. You have me on more meds than I can handle. I'm a zombie. I feel numb from them. Ryan came home and told me how I should be grieving and when I didn't agree with him he hit me, TWICE! I got up, left the house, and as I drove down the road the tree just suddenly seemed like the answer to all my prayers. I punched the gas and went for it. I sure as shit didn't think I'd end up here with you," I exasperate.

I watch as his pencil moves frenziedly across his pad. Not the right answer, I realize. I need to give him all the right answers so I can get the hell out of here when the time comes. "I'm sorry, Dr. Rand. I'm really frustrated right now," I backtrack.

"I can see that, Elle."

"I want to heal. I want to get through physical therapy and then I want to go home," I lie.

"I'm not sure it's going to be that simple," he retorts.

"Why not? How else does one get out of these places?"

"You have some serious work ahead of you and until you are deemed mentally stable. Ryan has Power of Attorney, meaning you can't sign yourself out," he explains.

"I will do the work. I will be cleared as mentally stable," I state. I am not giving the state of my mental health and life over to Ryan. I will do whatever it takes. Then it dawns on me, if he has POA, he has access to my funds. *All of my funds.* "Dr. Rand, what happens if I'm cleared and Ryan doesn't agree? Can he ask that I be monitored further? Held longer?"

"I suppose that could happen, yes." he lets on, making my breath falter. I suddenly feel woozy.

"I don't feel well. I think maybe I need to rest," I tell him. He lets me know that he will be back in three days for another appointment and leaves. Ryan now has a pretty sweet motive for keeping me hostage here. I am going to have to play nice with him. The blows just keep coming.

The next two weeks seem to move at a slug's pace. Slowly but surely I am able to move about on my own with a motorized wheelchair that has a joystick so I can control it with my right hand. The left side of my body frustrates me, both the leg and arm useless in their casts. Ryan doesn't bother coming to visit. Rachel lets me know that they haven't even received a phone call from him to check in on me. Part of me is happy at the news. I don't want him in my life. I don't want him near me. The other part of me knows that I need to get him in here and soon before he blows all my money, before it's too late to fix this. It takes all the energy I have to make it through each day. I'm trapped in this prison of crazy people with no end date in sight. My gut clenches in knots thinking about it. Is it possible to go crazy from being surrounded by crazy all day?

"Good afternoon, Elle. How are you today?" Dr. Rand asks.

"Feeling pretty good."

"Nice to hear. So shall we?" He asks.

"Sure." As if I have a choice.

"Last session you mentioned that Jenny helped you face some of your fears."

"Uh huh."

"I'd like to discuss those." He pushes.

"It wasn't really fears as much as things that I either wanted to do or didn't have the courage to do, I guess."

"Like what?" He prompts.

"Ummm, like throwing a drink in someone's face," I stammer.

"Really?" He clearly finds this interesting judging from the tone of his voice.

"Well, it's something that takes balls to do. I can't actually imagine doing it or what would happen afterwards but yeah.... I guess if I were a badass it could happen."

"Fascinating." He makes some notes on his pad. I hate that pad.

"Not really," I mutter.

"Tell me something else."

"Ok, going to dinner - out- alone."

"You've never eaten at a restaurant alone?" he inquires.

"No."

"Why not?"

"It would be awkward. People would judge me, wonder if I was stood up or why I wasn't with someone," I shrug.

"And why does that matter?" he pushes.

"I don't know, it just does," I say, frustrated.

"Elle, let's make a list."

"Of?"

"Of all these things that you feel matter. That if you had the chance, you'd like to see if you can accomplish just to say you did."

"Ahhh, okay, sure."

"Great. So we have 'Throwing a drink in someone's face' and 'eating dinner alone.' Yes?"

"Yeah."

"And... these two things stem from perceived social judgment?"

"I guess."

"Let's get two more on the list today," he says. I stop for a moment and think of things Jenny and I used to talk about.

"Learn to fight and ahh... sing karaoke," I tell him.

"Let's address 'learn to fight' first."

"Okay." He stares at me for a moment. "Oh! Right, you want me to talk about it. Well, I think it would be fun to learn boxing or kickboxing or MMA. But to actually go take a class or have a trainer for that kind of sport intimidates me and makes me self-conscious."

"Why?"

"I guess because I might not be good enough or I might fail at it."

"So another failure issue," he prompts.

"Sure," I reply. He nods again, jotting down more notes.

"Karaoke?"

"I sang in the chorus growing up, but in a group your voice blends in ...you can still hide. I guess karaoke would be making it about me. I could be booed off the stage because they think I'm terrible. Crowds always judge the person singing."

"Judgment and failure again. Quite the theme here, don't you think?"

"I think a lot of people might have these thoughts on these things so far. It's not abnormal."

"I didn't say anything about abnormal, Elle," he retorts. I huff in frustration at him.

"Is our time up for today?"

He winks at me and sets his pencil to rest. "I suppose it is. I'll see you in a few days. Have some more ready for the list," he says.

PRESENT

ELLE

DAY 12

My eyes are puffy and bloodshot and I feel as though I didn't sleep at all last night. Instead of going to the gym I opt for wallowing in my own misery for the morning. Colin doesn't call to find out why I didn't show and I don't call to offer up an explanation. I'm not sure how to tell him that I want to continue seeing him. I want to tell him that I really do feel the same things he does but after my gaff yesterday words fail me.

My thoughts are depressing and spiraling out of control. I know that all I have to do is pick up the phone and call him. I just have to pick up the phone. I'm such a coward though. What if he thought about it all night and decided that I'm fickle and untrustworthy? What if he yells unkind things at me? I don't want either of those outcomes to be how I remember him if I've ruined this. *Do something, Elle!* I just have to do something. I debate back and forth with myself about the pros and cons of just sending a text, calling, or showing up at his apartment. All options leave me too nervous. I settle on writing a note and sliding it under his apartment door. Then I can pretend, if I never hear from him again, that he never got it. What is wrong with me?

"Colin-

I'm an idiot and a coward. I do know what I want. I do trust you.

If I gave you my hand would you take it because my heart couldn't

beat one more minute without you.

If you don't hate me I'll be at the Wyngate Hotel lobby tonight at 6.

Elle"

I reread my note a hundred times before just deciding it's good enough. Clear and to the point. It's eleven and Colin should still be at the gym with a client today so I fold the note in half and walk to his apartment. After sliding it under his door I feel that whoosh of anxiety. The kind when you want to reach your hand back in and pull the note out just to avoid the rejection that could come with leaving it. I have no choice now, though. The walk back is torturous. I think maybe that I still need therapy. *Jenny, is this what normal people feel when they're in love? Is this that anguish that accompanies a broken heart? I've never felt this before and I don't even know if we were even really ever anything together. AHHHHHHH! Just once you could send me a sign, you know!*

Normally I don't mind being alone. I enjoy it. I like the quiet. I like having myself only to worry about but now, something's changed. He has filled that place in me that needed someone, becoming a mainstay in my life, friend, and the one I feel safest with. As I pass The Freaky Bean I notice Jenna exiting the cafe.

"Hey Elle!" Her smile drops as she takes in my face.

"Hi, Jenna."

"What happened to you? You look like me after a bad date." Her comment makes me chuckle. Apparently there is a look that screams relationship woes.

"I think I messed up. Big time," I confess.

"I'm on my lunch break, need to talk?" she offers.

"Oh no, I don't want to impose."

"Elle, don't be silly. Let's hear it- I'll even treat you to a cinnamon roll." She gestures back inside the cafe and I can't help it, those cinnamon rolls are the best.

"Deal. But my treat....for subjecting you to my gloom," I say, making her laugh. We head back inside to order and grab a table.

"Spill it," she pushes once we're settled.

"I've been seeing this guy, Colin. He's wonderful and amazing and ...and... the best thing that's ever happened in my life," I start. "And things were going great. Really. We have this weird connection. It was instantaneous. It scared me. I thought we were moving too fast..."

"Wait," she cuts me off. "How long have you been seeing each other?"

"Oh, ah, like ten days or so."

"Okay, well, that is quick...but go on."

"I told him after a perfectly lovely day, that I didn't think it was working and about moving too quickly and he got frustrated and told me he refused to give me up but then I bolted from the car when he dropped me off and I was supposed to train with him still this morning but blew it off even though I realized last night that I do want him. Like, a lot. He hasn't called or anything today to find out why I missed out training session." I finish breathless and smack my hands against my face.

"Elle, relax. Everyone gets scared. It's natural. I'm sure if you just call and talk to him things will be fine," she softly chuckles. I groan and look up to her.

"I thought about that and then decided against it. So I slipped a note under his door telling him if he doesn't hate me to meet me tonight at the Wyngate lobby."

"What? Why there?"

"Oh, I have to play the piano in the lobby." I wave it off. "It's part of the list."

Her eyebrows draw together in confusion. "What list?" she questions, making me sigh in frustration.

"That's kinda how all this started. I have a list of things to do. During one of those things I met him. Then, after a date, he asked if he could do the things on my list with me. So we have."

"You might be the most exciting and interesting person I've met." She gushes candidly.

"What?" I squawk.

"Elle, seriously. You have this guy, who sounds wonderful and wants to do these mysterious list things with you and you leave romantic notes for him. I swear my life is so bland in comparison. Friday mornings reading here is the highlight of my week." I shake my head slowly at her but a smile creeps over my face.

"You have no idea," I laugh and just like that I feel like Jenna and I are destined for friendship.

"Well. Okay, so there's a note waiting for him. Does he have any cute friends?" She pushes.

"Yes, there's a note, and yes, actually, he has two really hot friends." I waggle my brows at her suggestively.

"Next list item I want in," she giggles.

"Deal. Well the piano thing tonight is the next one... but yes... after that."

"No way! I'm showing up tonight to see if he shows!" She squeals.

"Wait, what?" I laugh.

"What song will you play? If you're playing, you should play something for him."

"Shit! I didn't even consider that. I haven't played in ten years, the only thing I remember is 'Moonlight Sonata,'" I tell her.

"Ohhhh... that's dark and haunting and passionate. That's good enough. What time?"

"Will you really come?" I can't believe she'd be my wingwoman.

"Of course! I have to see how this plays out now."

"Fine. Six. I'm going to steal the piano at six. They don't know I'm playing. I just have to do it." I explain.

"This gets better and better. I love it!" she squeals as I blow out a breath. "Listen, I have to get back to work, but I'll meet you at the hotel just before six." She giggles.

"Alright. Sounds good," I tell her as we exit the cafe. She waves me off as she hustles down the sidewalk back to work. Now I just have to figure out what to wear and how to get enough piano time in without being kicked out before he shows. If he shows, I remind myself.

I'm a ball of nerves and it has little to do with hijacking the hotel's piano. As promised, Jenna is waiting just inside the lobby for me when I arrive.

"Ready?" she squeals.

"No! I'm a ball of nerves."

"Oh stop. I'm sure he will come."

"I'm glad one of us is," I quip.

I watch her as she talks to a woman in the lobby. She looks distressed and uneasy. Her hands keep running through her hair and her mouth forms a perfect pout. I was angry as hell this morning when she didn't show at the gym but I can't say I didn't expect that. I thought about calling to make sure she was safe a thousand times today but if she wanted space and distance I'd try like hell to give it to her.

The note killed me. When I read it I wanted to call her right then and tell her of course I don't hate her. I wanted to tell her more than that but I'm going to have to wait for her to get there. Ben's sitting at the bar with me so I don't do anything stupid, like go to her. I want this to be on her. I want her to want this, to want me. I need to stop trying to convince her.

"Dude. Chill. Your knee is going to take the bar top off."

"Sorry. I just want this to be over with already."

"You're such a woman," he teases. "Who's the hottie with her?"

"I have no idea." We watch as Elle casually walks up to the empty piano and discreetly slides on to the bench. Her friend edges towards us, stopping at the entrance to the bar, looking around. Quietly music pours from the piano. I recognize the tune she's playing. "Sonata No. 14" in C-sharp minor's haunting sound resonates through the lobby and into the bar. I leave my stool, stopping when I arrive next to her friend. Elle's fingers move gracefully across the keys, I had no idea she could actually play too. That little shit.

Hotel staff members are filing into the lobby from god knows where with questioning looks. It's a surreal experience as security is called and heads towards her all the while "Moonlight Sonata" is providing a soundtrack of sorts. When they reach her she looks up and immediately stops playing. One of the security guards leans into her and quietly says something to which she nods her head and begins to stand. She glances to her friend as she follows the guard towards the front doors but when she sees me she stops dead in her tracks. Her friend's head whips around to me and a giant smile covers her face.

"I knew it," she says under her breath. The guard lightly tags Elle's arm making her flinch, but she continues to follow him. I wave Ben over to me and Elle's mystery friend.

"Who are you?" I ask.

"Jenna."

"Jenna, this is Ben. Make nice. I have to go get her." I turn and jog out to the sidewalk to find her.

"Are you mad?" she breathes from behind me. I spin around to face her.

"What do you think?" The words come out rough and abraded.

"That you're going to save me," she says quietly.

I had an entire speech planned. I was so pissed I wanted to say so much, but her words hit me with such force that everything's forgotten. She looks up to me under thick black lashes, biting her luscious bottom lip and I'm a goner. I reach out, yanking her to me, the sigh she releases into my chest as her arms come around my waist tell me everything I need to know. Everything just changed. She won't hold back anymore. I squeeze her tighter still and kiss the top of her head.

"Dammit, Elle, never do that to me again."

"Noted," she quips. "Oh! Jenna!"

"I left her with Ben."

"Oh. I can't go back in..." she smiles sheepishly, " so you'll have to go get them."

"Done. Don't go anywhere." I smile at her before pushing back through the lobby doors to retrieve our friends.

PRESENT

ELLE

DAY 13 (technically)

"I still can't believe they banned you....kick you out, sure, but banned?!" Jenna squeaks.

"Yeah and why didn't you tell Colin you have hot friends?" Ben chuckles while gawking at Jenna.

"We didn't realize we were friends until today, that's why," Jenna quips. She's a real firecracker and I can't wait to hang out more. "So what's next on the list, Elle?"

"Ah, tomorrow I'm supposed to skinny dip in a pool after hours."

"What?!" Jenna screams, causing Colin and I to burst out laughing. We can see the wheels turning in Ben's head as he processes what I've said.

"We're so in!" he says more to Jenna than anyone else.

"It will be tomorrow in about twenty minutes," Colin adds.

"You can't be serious," I say flatly.

"Why not? It will be more fun with all of us."

"I'm not getting naked for strangers," Jenna chimes in.

"Once you see my torso you'll change your mind," Ben cracks with a wide grin, leaving us all staring wide-eyed at his overwhelming self-confidence. "What? It's true," he shrugs.

How the hell did I end up here? Jenny, when everyone strips- check out the guys! A little slice of heaven right here on Earth. Seriously though, why did we think skinny dipping was a good idea? After a hefty amount of coaxing from Ben and Colin, Jenna and I actually agreed to skinny dipping. It's well after one in the morning and I can barely keep my eyes open, but Ben insisted we drive twenty minutes out of town to a rinky-dink roadside motel and use their pool.

"This is stupid," I grumble, crossing my arms over my chest.

"It will be fun," Colin says and rubs his hand on my back. "Now strip." I look over to him in mock horror at his callousness but can't stop the giggle that bubbles up.

"Okay, Elle, I'm only doing this if you do. On the count of three?" Jenna suggests and sucks in a huge breath. My hands come to the hem of my shirt as I start the countdown. "One, two......THREE!" I whip the shirt over my head and shimmy out of my skirt at the speed of light before moving to my bra and underwear. Jenna and I enter the water, loudly, practically at the same time. My head pops up, scanning the deck for the guys.

"Where are they?" Jenna asks.

"It's too dark, I can't see anything. This water is freezing," I say through chattering teeth.

A large splash sends water cascading over our heads as Colin and Ben cannonball us in a surprise attack.

"Shhh Jenna! I didn't even get to see you naked yet! If you keep squealing like that you'll wake everyone here," Ben chastises her. Colin ducks under water and swims between my legs, bucking his back as he passes through and sending me up and above water to my belly. Ben squawks with delight at my expense before I'm able to submerge myself neck deep.

"Colin!"

"Yeah?" His wet hair dripping and boyish grin make it hard to be irritated.

"Do you want Ben to have firsthand knowledge of my boobs?!" He actually looks pained for a moment before answering. "Nope. Wasn't really thinking," he admits, to which I can't help but chuckle. Jenna and Ben are treading circles around each other looking like two lost puppies. Colin snags my waist, pulling me to him. My legs wrap around his waist and our wet bodies mold together. His hazel eyes pierce mine momentarily before I'm given the best kiss in history. Colin's kiss is like air, and I can't seem to get enough of it but before it can go any further he pulls away. "You're shivering." His arms move as rapidly as the water allows up and down my back, trying to warm me.

"It's okay."

"What're you doing?!" a man booms from the gate at the pool. "Pool's closed!"

The four of us burst out laughing and scramble to the edge of the pool. Jenna and I skip the underwear and try as best we can to tug on dry clothes over wet bodies while Ben and Colin quickly hoist their pants up, tag their shirts, and usher us to the car while yelling apologies to the man over their shoulders. By the time we're seated in the car we're all rolling with laughter.

"I haven't done anything like that in years!" Jenna laughs.

"Wanna come back to my place?" Ben asks her.

"You're impossible," she shakes her head.

"Is that a yes?"

"No."

"So yeah, then?"

"No!" Jenna and I both squawk at him together. He pouts but then leans into Jenna and whispers something in her ear making her giggle. I wonder if she will end up back at his place. Colin reaches over, lacing his fingers through mine. "Will you come back to my place?" His face is still glistening with pool water and that stupid dimple pops out, making his face just that much more handsome.

"Yes," I say softly and give his hand a squeeze.

PAST

2012
March

My second month I finally ask Rachel if I can call Ryan. He's the only authorized visitor I'm allowed. When I finally get through to him, the conversation is awkward and rushed. When he finally shows two days later after dinner I'm fuming with negligence.

"Elle," he quietly greets me.

"Ryan. Why don't you sit," I clip. He sits in the chair furthest from me, unable to make eye contact.

"So, how are you?"

"I've felt better." Sarcasm drips from my voice.

"Well, maybe next time you won't run your car into a tree," he sneers. The audacity of this man never fails to amaze me.

"Look, I don't want to fight," I tell him. His gaze hits the floor as he searches for something to say.

"Elle, I need you. I want you to come home still."

I swallow the bile rising in my throat and say, "I want that too." He looks surprised.

"I'm sorry about.... that night. I didn't know how to get you to snap out of it and I took it too far," he says. I want to scream and tell him that a couple of slaps to the face is the least of the terrible things he's done to me throughout the years but I don't, instead, "Yes. You did," is what falls from my mouth. "But listen, we can talk about us later... I need to know that you've been paying the bills. Did you find the log-ins ok?"

"Of course I've been paying the bills, Elle." He grits out.

"I wasn't sure. I'm the one who's always taken care of that stuff," I say, trying to calm him.

"I'm not a child. I can pay a few bills," he spits.

"Okay. I just wanted to make sure you found the log-in page in the desk drawer." He stands from the chair and comes to the bed. When he reaches out and takes my hand I'm unsure what to do. "Listen, I have to go but I'll come back to visit over the weekend, yeah?"

"Oh," I mumble. "Yeah, that's fine."

"Should I bring you anything?" He asks, clearly an afterthought.

"Could you bring my iPod and Kindle, I get a little restless with just the TV all day." I ask hopefully.

"Sure," he says, his voice annoyed and put-out. He drops my hand and leaves. No kiss, not that I want one, no hug, nor do I want one of those. It seems though that he's not even trying to fake it anymore. I know everything he doesn't want me to. He's like poison working its way slowly through me and I don't think he'll give up until he's sure I'm done.

The next few sessions with Dr. Rand are spent digging at my marriage. I want to explain Ryan to him but I'm not sure he's really on my side. I think maybe he's team Ryan. He does of course, probably out of doctoral duty, agree with me that hitting another person is absolutely wrong. Without telling him directly about the years of verbal battery, I hint at the fact that my self-worth is seriously lacking due to things Ryan has directly said or done. For instance, that if Ryan had a list, I wouldn't be at the top of it. I am not a priority. Also that my list we've been working on would be thought frivolous. I can almost hear Ryan's voice complaining that he wasn't getting what he paid Dr. Rand for.

Dealing with the loss of my sister proves harder for me to talk about. I let it slip that I ask her for guidance once in a while. He had a field day with that one. Why do you think you talk to your dead sister? Does she answer you? Ugh. I didn't tell him that sometimes I think I do hear her or at least get a sign from her. I obviously lie and tell him that of course I don't hear voices and that isn't it natural - if you don't believe in God- to look up to the "heavens" and talk? I think I stumped him with that one. How is it sane to talk to God but not a person you actually knew?

Jenny. I miss her so much. I would never be in this situation if she was alive. I cry over her frequently still. I've asked to be weaned off the antidepressants and anti-anxiety pills because I'm so closely monitored here that if I can get along without them I'd prefer that. So far no one's said that we can't try that so I'm hopeful. Mostly at night, I stare out my window and ask Jenny how the hell I get out of this mess. So far, there's no answer.

PAST

May

As month four wraps up I find that the hole in my heart is slowly starting to close up. Talking, however indirectly, to my sister helps a lot. It's comforting to think she's watching over me and at the very least listening to me. Daily group therapy for grief and loss has actually managed to help me a lot. Most times I sit and silently listen, it's rare for me to speak. I take away what I can and leave the rest in the recesses of my mind. Ryan has visited four times since I've come out of a coma. Things are extremely tense between us when he does visit. I try to keep him close enough to gain any information I can but far enough that I don't lose my mind thinking about my life with him.

My casts come off today and for that I am thankful. My arm and leg both look sickly when they remove them. Grayish and scaly. The muscles in them are barely visible anymore. I start physical therapy next week. In the meantime, Dr. Rand tells me that although they are still concerned that I could be a threat to myself I have new privileges. I now get to hang in the common room with all the other crazies on this floor. At least it's a change of pace from being stuck motoring down the hallway or in my room.

"Hi, Sugar. How are ya tonight?" Manny asks me. He's a medtech who brings me my pills every night at nine.

"Good thanks. You?"

"I'm pretty good. Won a pretty little pile of money at poker last night." Every Wednesday Manny plays poker and every Thursday night I hear about his winnings or losses. He's a jovial guy who makes me smile. He hands me my little white cup of pills and then my little cup of water. Just like every other night I put the pills in my mouth, we clink our white plastic cups, and I swallow.

"Looks like you're being reduced to a sleeping pill and a multivitamin starting next week. Congrats," he laughs.

"Gee, thanks. But yeah... I'm glad to be off this shit."

"Hold that chin up, Buttercup. Every storm runs out of rain." His words of encouragement makes my soul feel light.

"You're one of the good ones, Manny. You and Rachel."

"If all my patients were like you this job would be a breeze, Sugar." He picks up his tray, waves good night, and leaves, closing the door behind him.

Physical therapy kicks my ass. It's intense and grueling. By the end of every session I am beat but the muscle in my leg and arm are starting to look much better. It gives me something to do though so I try not to complain. After each session I sit in the common room, which reminds me of *One Flew Over the Cuckoo's Nest*. There are the window-starers, the people who mumble to themselves, the droolers, and the ones who rant and rave about anything and everything. There are only two other people who sit and people watch like I do.

One is a girl who can't be more than nineteen and looks desperately sad. It makes my heart hurt to look at her. The will to live is gone from her eyes. The other is a man who is probably in his late forties. Sometimes we sit together at a table and silently watch and judge all the other people. We all have yellow bands on our wrists so I know they too are on suicide watch. They color code us. It's embarrassing to say the least.

"Elle, you've come pretty far over the last five months," Dr. Rand says.

"Thanks." I force a smile. I still don't trust him.

"I suggested to Ryan that you would be ready for release, pending you continue therapy with me."

"You did?!" I can't hide the excitement in my voice.

"I did, yes." He pauses. "Ryan feels strongly though that during his visits with you, you are still despondent and withdrawn and he's concerned that maybe you need some more time." That's when it hits me. Ryan isn't going to let me out of here. Not anytime soon. I've been locked away on a psych ward for five and a half months and I'm not crazy. I'm not suicidal. I was lost before but I've had time away from Ryan and it's helped clear my head. I am going to be okay. I do want to live. I absolutely though do not want to live here in this locked-up hell. Regardless of how I feel about Dr. Rand's motives, he has aided me in working through some of my more overwhelming feelings.

"Oh?" I squeak.

"How do you feel about that?"

"What? His comment or staying longer?" I pose.

"Staying longer." He answers passively.

"Wait? Why do you automatically side with him? He's not here talking to me daily. He doesn't know." Panic is starting to take over my body. I need to get out of here.

"Well, his concerns are valid. You will be going back to the house where you live with him. If you are as he says around him that's something we need to address," he explains calmly as if it's no big deal. I could spit fire right now. Rage rips through me.

"Add slash a tire to the list, Doc." I push up from my bed and stomp to the common room. When I'm sure Dr. Rand has left my room I go back and sob until Manny comes to dose me for the night.

I will go crazy if I'm forced to stay here indefinitely. Will he always be able to come up with a reason that will buy me more time put away? Fear tears through me as I lay in my sterile bed in my sterile white room with a barred window that overlooks a parking lot. The bars on the window are depressing but considering we are only one story up it's probably to prevent escape attempts. *Jenny please... I'm begging you...How do I get out of here?* I hold my breath and wait until my lungs burn from the lack of oxygen.

I imagine I live in a small cottage on the ocean. I wake up late every morning and enjoy a cup of coffee on my little balcony. When I walk back in I shower and dress and go to work in the small florist shop I own. Flowers bring me joy. I send beautiful arrangements to people, hopefully brightening their day. When I get home at night I sit on that balcony and listen to the waves lap the sand and enjoy a glass of wine. No one yells at me. No one tells me I'm not good enough. No one bothers me. I'm free. I'm happy. I'm content.

I can hear Jenny's voice singing along to her favorite Dixie Chicks song, "As you wander through this troubled world in search of all things beautiful you can close your eyes when you're miles away and hear my voice like a serenade."

PRESENT

ELLE

DAY 14

After idly spending the better part of the day in bed, Colin and I finally pull ourselves together, ready to face another day. I'm happily lounging on his couch as he clicks away on his laptop.

"Hey, listen to this. Falcon Rec Department has a cooking class today that still has some openings. Learn to prepare the luscious, beautiful desserts you have enjoyed in fine restaurants, or those heartwarming homemade delights. We teach you to prepare the pastries, fillings, and icings. We will teach you not only how to prepare fabulous desserts, but also the pastries for savory hors d'oeuvre and main courses," he reads from the website.

"Mmmm that sounds like a good one. I never thought about a desserts class."

"Should we register?" He asks.

"What time is it at?" I yawn and stretch, trying to motivate myself.

"Four," he answers. I glance at the clock on the cable box. Two hours from now.

"Sure. Let's do it." Colin's fingers click and clack on the keys as I push myself off the couch and head to the shower. "I'll need to swing by my place for a change of clothes," I call over my shoulder.

"K!"

The recreation center is an old beat up looking school. The classroom we're in reminds me of my old high school science lab. Bland concrete walls painted an off-white that looks dirty. There are three other couples in here with us. An older couple who look blissfully happy together sit at one desk holding hands. To our left are two twenty-some-things that appear to be on a first or blind date together. They both sit quietly stealing glances at each other nervously. Across from the older couple are two women who are cackling about the delicious wine they had before coming to the class. Glancing over at Colin I notice he too is people watching, a small grin playing on his face as he listens to the two women laughing up front.

"Interesting mix."

"I was just thinking the same thing," he chuckles. "I think those two will make the class." He nods at the two wine-o's.

"I don't know, my bet's on the first date couple next to us," I whisper back. He glances over just as the guy reaches for his uncapped water bottle and somehow manages to knock it over, spilling water all over the table and his date's lap. The instructor walks in just as said date squeals in irritation.

"Okay, maybe you're right," he says under his breath.

"Good evening!" the instructor starts. "I'm Chrissy and tonight we'll be learning to make lemon and berry-filled

Danish pastries." As she moves around the room handing out instructions she continues, "Danishes can be found in so many fun and fanciful shapes. Some are better than others for showcasing a fresh filling, and this particular shape, called 'the envelope,' is perfect for cradling a big scoop of lemon curd and bright red strawberries. In the cabinets below your desks you should find everything you need." With that we're off.

Colin brings the water to a boil in a large saucepan while I whisk the sugar, cornstarch, and lemon zest together, then add the mixture slowly to the hot water, whisking constantly until mixed together. "My arm is burning... you take over," I complain. Danish making is hard work.

"Wuss," he teases, continuing to whisk until it comes to a boil and becomes very thick. The first date couple argues quietly over every little step. The guy throws his hands up in frustration and sits back on his stool, letting her take over.

Once we add about half of the hot mixture to the egg yolks, and whisk until it looks creamy, we carefully beat the warmed yolks into the pot and continue cooking and whisking until mixture comes to a boil.

"What now?" Colin asks.

"Um, let's see...add butter, lemon juice, zest and vanilla, and stir." I instruct.

"This is kinda fun."

"I just want to get to the taste-testing part." I sulk a little. My belly is rumbling from all the smells wafting around the room. I really could use a sugar hit right about now.

"Right, never come between Elle and her pastries," he says and winks.

Chrissy walks around the classroom every few minutes

praising or correcting the class's efforts. By the time we're spooning large dollops into the pastry envelopes my stomach is growling and my mouth is watering.

"Only fifteen more minutes," Colin whispers to my belly. I smack him playfully on the head and laugh.

At the end of class everyone gets to test out their Danishes. The older couple's looks perfect as they cut into it. The first date couple's looks like it exploded curd and filling everywhere and is burnt, the girl grumbling at the guy as he pulls it out. I think this will be their last date. The two women up front cooked theirs a little too long but are happily indulging in it anyways with their fingers. Colin cuts ours in half, picks up a piece, and feeds it to me.

"Ohmygodthistastessogood," I mumble inaudibly around the bite. Colin chortles at me before popping his half into his mouth.

"Thank you all so much for coming! Feel free to bring the recipe home with you and experiment with different fillings!" Chrissy says, ending the class excitedly. Colin folds the recipe in half and tucks it into his back pocket. As we file out of the classroom, Colin's hand at the small of my back, my train of thought moves to the older couple.

"I want to be like them someday," I express. Colin smiles, taking them in. They walk hand in hand down the hallway excitedly talking about making more Danishes at home.

"We are like them."

"I meant old and still in love."

"How do you know they didn't start off just like this?" He stops mid-step, leans down, and kisses me softly before continuing our walk.

"I guess I don't," I say and grin and push up on my toes to press a kiss to the underside of his jaw.

PRESENT

ELLE

DAY 15

I woke up early and left Colin sleeping in my bed. I took my coffee and a notebook to the deck and sat to think. I want to write a message that means something. If someone gets it someday, if it really washes up somewhere, I want it to inspire them. It's not as easy as it seems. Writing a simple message should be easy but I keep coming up with clichés or cheesy messages. Writing something from the heart when you can't find the right words to convey what you want is really irritating.

"Whatcha doin', Babe?" Colin kisses my neck before joining me at the table.

"I'm trying to write a message....but I'm frustrated. I can't think of anything worth writing."

"How do you know what's worth writing?"

"If I'm sending it out into the great big ocean and someone could find it someday I want it to be profound. Inspiring. Not lame and cheesy," I explain.

"Well, why don't you just start writing things that come

to mind. I'll do the same. Then we can read all the ideas and pick the two best ones."

"Are you always so diplomatic?"

"Are you always searching for perfection? Sometimes it doesn't have to be perfect, Elle."

I glower at him in irritation but secretly admit to myself that he has a point.

"Fine." We sit in silence writing for an hour before I'm ready to show him anything.

We deliberate so much that my head hurts before finally deciding on two messages.

"Jenny,

You were the most beautiful person. My wish is that I continue to follow your heart's desires and your dreams for me. I'm so grateful for the love and support you gave to me, the big sister. I promise to remember to love, and to have fun, and to never forget the feeling I have right now. This is for you. Your wish for love and happiness in my life, a wish for my future to shine as bright as yours did is coming true. I love you and miss you every day."

"Your smile is the only thing that matters."

Colin's convinced that my letter to Jenny is the way to go. That it's touching and hopeful and some stranger will smile reading it. Colin's is simple but moving. If a stranger got that I truly believe they would think it was a wonderful message. I like the simplicity of it so we roll the two pages up and grab the two empty wine bottles I've been saving. We stuff the rolled papers into our bottles before re-corking them and walking over the dune to the beach.

"This is it."

"Ready?" he asks.

"Go!" I shout excitedly. Gripping the neck of the bottle I hurl it as far as possible into the ocean. I laugh when Colin's goes much further out than mine. We stand next to each other hand in hand watching the bottles bob and float away with the tide. When the bottles drift out of sight he tugs on my hand gently.

"Ready?"

"For what?"

"Training. You haven't been in days."

"Let's go," I pout. He bends at the waist and kisses the pout right off my face. "We should call Jenna and see if she wants to train with me...Ben would be happy," I suggest as we make our way up the deck stairs and into the cottage.

"Ben and Jenna don't need our help. They are completely caught up in their own whirlwind right now."

"They are?!"

"Haven't you talked to Jenna?" He looks confused.

"Not since skinny dipping. I texted her but didn't get a reply."

"Well, Ben didn't get lucky that night, but he did the next," Colin laughs.

"Shut UP!" I squeal at him.

"Why do girls say that?"

"Whatever. I'm calling her as soon as we're done at the gym."

Three hours later after a brutal fight between me and the hanging bag and a sparring round with John I'm finally able to beat Ben into submission over what happened the other night. When we leave the gym I'm so excited for Jenna that I can't contain it anymore and call her immediately.

"How could you not tell me?!" I practically scream into the phone when she picks up.

"Hi, Elle. I'm great, thanks for asking," she laughs.

"I'm sure you are, now...details!"

"I'm still at work. How 'bout we meet up for dinner and I'll tell you all about it."

"Time and place."

"Blitz at seven."

"I'll be there!" I squeal before hanging up.

"You know, you're awfully adorable when you're excited," Colin chortles.

"I am?"

"Yup. Now, let's go home and enjoy some afternoon delight before dinner." He waggles his brows at me.

"You got it big boy!" I blurt before bursting out laughing.

PAST

2012

July

Month six is slowly passing and showing no signs of speeding up. Dr. Rand says that in another two months he will talk to Ryan about releasing me again. I have no hope that I will be out of here in two months. Ryan has stopped visiting altogether. When I ask the good doctor what he thinks about that, he evades the question, instead asking me how I feel about it. I beg my sister every night for a sign. My list with Dr. Rand has grown to thirty things. It seems like a waste now to continue on with it since I don't foresee getting to tackle any of them in the real world.

"Hi, Honey, why the frown?" Manny asks. Must be nine already.

"Just thinking," I say.

"Buck up, Buttercup."

"Did you win last night?"

"As a matter of fact I did." He smiles.

"Good for you, Manny." He sets the tray down, hands

me my pills, we cheers our cups, and I swallow down my salvation. The sleeping pill is the only reason I sleep lately.

"Night, ElleBell," he waves.

"Night." He shuts the door behind him when it hits me. Escape. All I have to do is escape.

For the next six nights I place my pills under my tongue, swallow my water, and when Manny leaves I take the sleeping pills and stash them in my pillowcase, careful to relocate them on laundry day. On the third day I nicely ask Dr. Rand for a copy of the list that we've made thus far. After assuring him and Rachel that I won't off myself with paper cuts, they let me keep the photocopied piece of paper taped to my wall. On the fourth day I manage to sneak a plastic bag from the trashcan at the nurses' station into my room. After Manny leaves the sixth night I take all the pills from the pillowcase, put them into the plastic baggy and crush them into a fine white powder, using one of my crutches that I no longer need.

It's Friday, the seventh day. I'm sitting on my bed as always when Manny enters, carrying the tray of cups and pills. When he reaches the side of the bed he sets the tray on the sliding table between us, pulls the pills and our two white cups of water off the tray, and sets them aside.

"Hey, Buttercup. How's things?" he asks. I feel like shit for what I'm about to do. I really like Manny.

"Things are status quo," I tell him. He smiles at me, picks up my pills, and reaches out to hand them to me.

"Ahh. I think there's a mistake." I never complain so he stops short. "Dr. Rand and I are working on my sleep cycle and were going to try a week with no sleeping pills. I think I'm supposed to be on multivitamin only tonight," I say, trying to keep my eyes from darting all over the room.

"Huh? I didn't see anything about that," he says.

"Would you mind checking? Please? If I don't comply with the good doctor I end up in here longer," I plead.

"Sure thing, Sugar." He smiles, picks up the tray, leaving our two waters and my pills sitting on the table and walks out of the room. I quickly tag the plastic baggy from under my pillow and empty the contents into the water cup that he will use. I swish my finger around in it to try and make it dissolve faster. I yank my finger out and try to dry quickly on the leg of my pajama pants. The knob clicks and Manny walks in.

"Sorry, Elle, he must have forgotten to make a note. You'll have to take it tonight. I'll write a note in your chart telling Dr. Rand so you don't get in trouble," he says and smiles at me.

"Okay. Thanks, Manny. So, did you win last night?" I ask, putting the pills in my mouth.

"You know it!" he says excitedly. We pick up our cups, cheers them, and with smiles on our faces drink our water shots.

"Night, Sugar." We wave goodbye and he leaves. I dart to the bathroom and spit the pills into the toilet before peeing and flushing. Now for the hard part: waiting.

I wait an hour. I pace around my room frantically, trying to figure out how exactly to explain all this when the time comes. My heart feels like it might explode out of my chest. If I do this, there will be no turning back. Ryan will lose it. I know without a doubt he will do everything in his power to hunt me down. I'll need to be smart. My anxiety is through the rough thinking and over thinking all of the outcomes that could happen. At ten p.m. I crack my door and peer over to the nurses' station. Manny's head is on the desk, his body slumped over. The rise and fall of his ribs slow and steady. Sleeping. This is it.

The list! I can't forget the list. I rip it from the wall fold it up and stuff it in my sports bra. My heart is beating wildly in my chest. I feel frantic and I'm starting to sweat. I pull on my hoodie sans hood strings of course, slip my feet into my lace-less Keds and make my way to Manny's sleeping form.

It's eerily quiet in the corridor right now. Just the faint hum of the ice machine and various beeps and buzzes from patients' rooms. I quietly sneak around the nurses' station desk and crouch down to Manny. I'm so sorry. I really do like you. Please forgive me. I tug his wallet out of his back pocket and remove all the cash. A hundred dollars will be plenty to tide me over until the morning. I stuff the cash in my sports bra. I unclip Manny's employee badge from the front of his shirt, toss the wallet on the desk next to his head and quickly walk down the hall.

I did it. A wave of relief washes over me leaving me temporarily giddy. When I exit the store I notice a few taxis parked waiting across the street. I make my way over to them. "Could you take me to a cheap hotel?" I ask through the open window to the cabby.

"How cheap?"

"Dirt cheap," I reply. He nods his head at me and I open the back door and climb in. He drives four blocks before pulling up in front of a dilapidated brick building. "They rent by the hour," he informs me. I didn't mean this cheap but honestly it will do. I hand him a ten-dollar bill and get out of the car. When I finally check in, paying for one night, I'm left with fifty-two dollars and change. The cab ride to my house from here will be at least thirty dollars. I lie down on top of the blankets fully clothed and stare at the chipping ceiling. *Jenny, we did it. I'm out. Almost free. Stay with me.* An hour later I fall asleep.

I wake with a start. I'm groggy and can't remember where I am. It's disorienting. When my brain catches up with me I let out a squeal of joy. This is the dirty, cheap hotel. I am not in my sterile white room at St. Francis. I escaped.

PAST

At eight I check out and flag down a cab. "303 Westerly Road," I tell him. The drive takes us twenty minutes outside the city. The closer we get the more my palms sweat. He better be at work. I keep having hot flashes and my stomach rolls with each mile closer we get. When we finally pull up onto my street, I'm a ball of nerves and anxiety-ridden. What if he's home, then what? As we pass my house relief washes over me. His car isn't there. I instruct the cab driver to pull over two houses down and to wait for me to come back. I pull the door handle and swing the door open. Mrs. Potter is watering the flowers in her front yard. I give a wave and walk down the sidewalk to my house.

I don't bother trying the door. It will be locked. I grew up in this house though and know all the easy ways to get around a locked door. I pull the screen from the casement window and pull the edge of the window until I can reach my arm in far enough to crank it open the rest of the way.

After I slip inside the guest room I stand by the door and wait. It's dusty and clean in here because we never have guests. If I do this, really do this, everything changes forever. I turn the knob and step into the hall. My legs are shaking badly and it takes all my effort to suck breaths in and out of my lungs.

Upstairs I change into a summer dress and ditch the Keds in the back of the closet as I grab a pair of sandals. I throw handfuls of summer clothes, shoes, and other necessities into my suitcase. There's a bra that doesn't belong to me on the floor next to the bed. The sight of it makes my stomach roll but I push on. When I feel I've got everything I'll need for the time being I zip it shut and carry it to the desk downstairs. Setting the suitcase to the side I start to dig through the side drawer of my desk. When I locate my passport and checkbook, I toss them into the front pocket of my bag.

Turning to scan the living room I notice we already have a new giant flat screen TV hanging on the wall complemented by a new stereo system sitting shelved under it. Ryan's been busy, that's probably not the only new purchase. The house is a wreck. Beer bottles, discarded clothes, and empty take-out containers are strewn everywhere. My instinct is to pick it all up quickly before leaving. It's a habit that's kept his monstrous side at bay many times. I shove the feeling away though. He can't know I was here and I don't owe him anything. I need time to get away without tipping him off.

I take a deep breath, curl my fingers around the handle of the suitcase and leave through the back door, making sure to lock the handle again before shutting it. With my suitcase rolling behind me I walk back to the cab. "First National Bank on Pleasant Street, please," I tell him.

Entering the bank makes me nervous. People know me here. They knew my parents and my sister and now probably know Ryan. I sit in a chair, suitcase next to me, and wait for a representative to come out. "Hi, Mrs. Darling, what can we do for you today?" a man whose name tag reads "Robert" greets me.

"I need to make a large withdrawal." I follow him to his desk and sit.

"That's a hefty sum to walk around with," he states as he looks over my account on his monitor.

"Yes, I'm aware, but it needs to be done. Leave three thousand in the account." I shouldn't leave him anything but a small part of me can't seem to just leave him high and dry. I hand him my passport and checkbook as proof of identification and he gets started.

By the time he's finished the manager has joined us and is asking questions that are starting to alarm me. I don't have time for this.

"Is everything all right, Mrs. Darling? We don't generally advise customers to walk out of the bank with a hundred and fifty thousand dollars," the manager says as he eyes me suspiciously.

"Everything is fine, thank you. If we could be quick about this I'd appreciate it." Thirty minutes later I exit the bank with a large deposit bag full of cash zipped inside my suitcase. The cab the bank called for me is waiting at the door.

"Bus station please," I tell the driver as I close the door.

I'm standing in line at the ticket counter trying to decide where to go. Just as I take my place at the window I decide on a little seaside town about three hours south of here. "One ticket to Searsport please."

"Round trip?"

"One way."

"That's thirty-three dollars," he says. I had him a fifty and wait for my change and the ticket.

The bus doesn't leave for an hour so I'm stuck sitting in one of the uncomfortable chairs in the waiting area. My knee bounces uncontrollably as I wait. I grab a bag of chips from the vending machine. The TV hanging in the corner is set to the local news station. Across the bottom the news ticker scrolls updated news stories. "Local woman: Elle Darling, escaped St. Francis Hospital last night. If seen call 843-543-5555." A picture of me from Jenny's funeral flashes across the screen. My face is gaunt and lifeless in the picture. I look around the waiting area but all eyes are on books, phones, magazines, or travel companions. I sit back down keeping my eyes on the floor. I need to be on that bus.

If anyone on the bus recognizes me no one says anything. I sit at the back using my suitcase to keep the seat next to me vacant. The three-hour bus ride is boring and mostly highway with the occasional glimpse of the ocean. Every time someone gets up and walks to the bathroom I think they're coming for me, that they recognize me from the news. Damn Ryan for putting a picture of me up.

I walk away from the bus dragging my suitcase behind me and head straight for the line of cabs out front. I hop in the first available one, keeping my suitcase with me in the backseat. Searsport is a decent-sized city on the water. The small downtown district is charming, lined with shops and offices. The cabby lets me off at Jowett and Cutler's law firm. I walk through the glass double doors into the lobby.

"Hi," I greet the receptionist.

"Hello. How can I help you today?" she asks and smiles.

"I need to make an appointment with one of the attorneys," I tell her.

"Okay." She hits a few keys on the keyboard as I wait. "The first available appointment I have is Tuesday at one. Will that work?" she asks.

"Perfect."

"Your name?"

"Jenny Parks," I say. I know it's a lie but I don't want my name to spark any recognition until I can meet with the lawyer.

"Okay Jenny, I just need your contact information and then we'll be set."

I falter for a moment. "I ah, I don't have a cell phone or a place to stay just yet," I say and shuffle my feet nervously.

"I could recommend a hotel for you. As long as we can contact you at the hotel that should be fine," she says.

"That would be wonderful." Half an hour later I have a beachfront cottage at the Waterford Inn for the month.

"When you get there, you'll need to pay and change the reservation to just your name," the receptionist informs me.

"Thank you." I say humbly.

I exit the office wheeling my suitcase behind me. It's a beautiful sunny day. The air smells like the saltwater. I glance over the directions to the Inn again and start walking. Two blocks down is a CVS. I buy myself a box of "Mahogany" hair dye before continuing on to the Inn.

Once I check in and settle into my tiny one room cottage I open the box of hair dye in the bathroom and get to work coloring my honey blonde hair. Thirty minutes later I am officially a brunette. The color works on me. It doesn't look unnatural and it actually makes my eyes pop more. Maybe I'll keep it for a while.

The cottage is quaint. It's one great room with a small galley-type kitchen that runs along one wall. The rest of the room is open. There is a dining nook to the side of the kitchen and then it's all living room. There's a comfortable-looking couch and two armchairs that face glass French doors that swing out to a small deck that has a view of the ocean. Stairs off the deck lead down to a small patch of grass and just beyond that there's a path through the dunes leading to the beach. I already adore it. The bedroom is maybe ten-by-ten and houses a single full-sized bed and one dresser. The bathroom is off the bedroom and simply has a shower, sink, and toilet. It's all that I'll need. If I open the bedroom window I can hear the tide crashing against the sand. It's peaceful.

A few hours later I venture out to the little main drag and buy myself a new prepaid cell phone, a radio, and a used Kindle. For the next three days I sit on the beach or my deck and I read and listen to music in peace and sunshine. It feels good to be alone. It feels good to exist for me only. And each morning when I wake up I feel a little more whole. At night I bask in the glory of concocting meals for myself and experimenting with ingredients. I'll be honest, some of them are terrible and I end up eating a bowl of cereal instead. But with my little radio wafting music into the open space and me free to do and try as I please, I experience joy for the first time in a long time.

Jenny, can you see me? Can you see my happiness? I want you to know how content I feel right now. I want you to know you were right. I could, and I did do it. I wish you were here with me.

DAY 16

Dinner with Jenna was a blast. Blitz might be my new favorite place. We gossiped about her and Ben's fledgling relationship, had an amazing dinner, and drank too many martinis. Ben, John, and Colin had a boys' night but by ten Colin and Ben were blowing up our phones, wanting to meet up so we all got together at The Lounge, a new club Jenna had wanted to check out. After a night of dancing our butts off and a drunken walk back to the cottage, Colin and I had collapsed into bed, immediately falling asleep.

After a late breakfast and an even later training session at the gym, Colin surprises me by telling me that he took it upon himself to sign us up for a private ballroom dance lesson. I'm so excited I can hardly contain my glee. At his command we dress up and he takes me out to dinner before our lesson, making a special date night out of it.

My heels echo on the hardwood floor of the empty dance studio. The old mill makes a beautiful place for a studio. Floor-to-ceiling windows run along one wall and the other wall is all mirrors. From a door at the opposite end, a short man walks out.

"You must be Colin!" he claps his hands together as he makes his way to us.

"Yes, nice to meet you," Colin returns.

"Who's this lovely thing you brought with you?"

"Hi. I'm Elle."

"Larry, nice to meet you, aren't you lucky to be with this tall drink of water," he says and winks at me. Colin shuffles his feet nervously before Larry pulls a nip out of his back pocket.

"I find that the men usually need a shot to loosen up."

Colin's grin grows wide as he takes the nip and chugs it.

"Thanks," he chortles.

"Okay, let's get started then! Face your partner and stand close together--close enough that your torsos are touching," Larry says and positions us.

"I like this," Colin grins devilishly at me.

"Colin, place your right hand on the middle of Elle's lower back. Extend your left hand out to your side with your arm bent and grasp her right hand in a loose grip. On the first beat, walk forward slowly with your left foot, placing down your heel first and then your toes. Elle will mirror each of your movements on every beat throughout the dance."

The music starts and Larry guides us through the moves he just explained. On the second beat, we step forward, slowly slinking forward together followed by stepping forward quickly and immediately sliding our feet quickly to the right. We practice this a few times until we're comfortable with it before moving on. I love the way Colin's body cradles mine. The heat he gives off.

"Great! Now, shift your weight to your left foot and do a right forward rock step: while making a half-turn clockwise, step forward quickly on your right foot, and then quickly shift your weight back to your left foot. With your right foot, slowly step forward to complete the half turn."

"Ah what?" Colin stops moving us, completely confused. Larry laughs at our flabbergasted faces and walks us through the rest slowly. After running through the moves almost ten times we finally nail it and move around the floor seductively together in a real tango. My body buzzes with excitement as we dance.

"This is awesome!" I squeal. "I feel like one of those professional dancers being swept all over the floor by you." Colin's only response is a shit-eating grin as he keeps me pressed tightly to him and continues to move us to the music.

Our lesson was quite possibly the most fun I've had in a long time. The closeness of the moves, the way he led me around the floor, and the fact that he too enjoyed himself has my heart beating wildly in my chest. Joy. Unadulterated joy. Unbuckling my seatbelt, I lean across the middle console of the car and start trailing kisses from his ear down to his neck.

"What's gotten into you?" he smirks.

"You make me feel, Colin. I don't want the past to define me anymore."

"It doesn't define you. You define you." He puts the car in park and turns to me. "You've been doing all these things, we've been doing them. Do you realize that we've done more together in two weeks than most couples do in a lifetime? We fit, Elle. I want you to enjoy me. I love seeing you carefree and happy."

"I need to thank your mom," I blab, causing him to treat

me to one of his dimples and a deep belly laugh. It's such a turn-on seeing him so happy and content.

I crawl into his lap, my butt beeping the horn accidentally in the process, and kiss him like the world is ending. Our kiss soon becomes frenzied and desperate. We can never seem to get close enough to each other. I pop the door handle, spilling us out of the car; his mouth is gentle as he kisses me below the slope where my neck and shoulder meet. We barely make it into the cottage before clothes are flying and I'm in his arms, legs wrapped at his waist. He stumbles back, smashing me into the wall but that doesn't break our kiss. His erection presses between my legs and I think I'll go insane with need if he doesn't take me soon. "Colin," I pant, "I need you." He adjusts his hips and slams into me.

There are no words for the pleasure it brings me. Pounding into me with lust-lidded eyes, he reaches one hand between us and finds the one spot that drives me insane. I don't have time to catch my breath from his lascivious kisses before a strangled groan tears from my throat and I'm twisted tighter until I'm coming. Wave after wave of earth-shattering tsunamis break over me until I can't cling to him anymore. I never understood what it felt like to both desire and feel desired before now. He carries all my weight with ease, finishing moments after I do. Sliding down the wall to the floor in a mess of body parts he murmurs in my ear, "The things you do to me." His words make me tremble, not in fear, but in knowing that he's crazy about me. Every action matches every word he speaks to me. He shows me nothing but love and kindness. He gazes at me as if I were the center of his world. It's a heady feeling. His fingers draw lazy patterns up and down my arms for a spell until we're forced to move from the unforgiving hardwood floor to somewhere more comfortable.

DAY 17

"So I think today we should go for a drive down the coast-line. What do you think?" I ask post-workout.

"Sounds like a good idea, did you have anywhere in mind?"

"Hmmm... I don't know." I roll my eyes upward and tap my pursed lips in thought.

"Elle? What's up your sleeve?"

"Come see!" I yelp with excitement. This morning Colin had an early client so I had time to pull off the best surprise. I drag him behind me outside and wait for him to notice something.

"Elle?"

"What's strange about the street right now?" I ask and watch as he glances up and down the street until his eyes finally rest on a bright yellow Ferrari.

"Is that a..."

"YES!" I cut him off. He looks like a kid on Christmas

morning, jumping around wildly, eyes bugging out and squealing like a little girl.

"Can I drive it?!" he asks, still gaping at me.

"Yes, you can drive down the coast if I can drive back..." I barter.

"Whatever you want! Holy shit this is going to be the best day ever!" He's still screeching and I can't help but roll with laughter at his response.

"Okay, we have to shower if you want to ride in this thing... come on, big guy," I say, tugging his hand. He shakes his head a few times like he's trying to wake up from a dream before following my lead and hitting the locker room.

The car is stunning in the flesh, as you'd expect, the interior finds a new level of elegance and class with hand-stitched leather combined with brushed aluminum. It's gorgeous. What this beast does best is get you all hot and bothered, making you write bad checks, and leaving you gasping and clutching, trying to explain to your new friends--the South Carolina State Troopers--why temptation was impossible to resist. I cannot wait to sit my ass in that immaculate piece of machinery next to my amazing girl and go for a ride.

When Elle and I finally fold into the Ferrari, and I swear she took extra-long getting showered and dressed today just to torment me, I am so giddy I actually stall the car twice just trying to start it. Only slightly embarrassed at my gaff, I poke fun of myself. "Third time's a charm right?"

"Sure, Rico," she laughs. God, I love that fuckin' laugh she has.

"Did you actually just reference Rico Suave?" I tease.

"Yep. I sure did!"

Turning the key once more while clutching this time I almost come in my pants as the engine comes to life. I swear the car actually purrs. I put her in gear and we shoot down the street. I like the feeling of the sudden acceleration but anything with an engine capable of launching the car to sixty-two miles an hour in less than four seconds and topping it out at almost three hundred and twenty klicks is not exactly a Sunday-drive-to-meeting station wagon. Elle is squealing with delight as we speed towards Route 17. Outside of meeting Elle, this might be the highlight of my life. Heads turn, women stare, hell, even men stare as we blow past them looking sexy as hell.

"Faster!" Elle yells over the engine. Her face is lit up like the Fourth of July. I gently press on the gas pedal and we shoot forward, gravity pressing us both into our seat backs. The sun reflects off the ocean sparkling to our left and the saltwater breeze only adds somehow to the exhilaration of the moment. For the next hour we speed along the coast taking in the sights and enjoying the ride.

"Do you want to stop and grab a bite while we're here?" I ask as we enter Charleston.

"There's supposed to be a great new place I read about."

"Here?"

"Yeah, Husk, I think it was on Queen Street," she says.

"Let's see if we can find it."

After getting lost twice we finally find our way to Queen Street and find parking with some ease. The restored Victorian house's relaxed atmosphere is alluring as we walk up the front porch. The smells wafting from the windows already have my mouth watering.

"It smells delicious," Colin declares while we're waiting to be seated.

"Agreed. I can't believe we're here. The picture I saw in the write up doesn't do this place justice. It's awesome." The atmosphere is comfortable and laid-back with true Southern charm oozing from every nook and cranny. Colin orders the shrimp and grits with tomato-braised peppers and surry sausage and I get heritage pork with smoky field peas and kale.

When our meals arrive we barely talk. The food is astoundingly good. We're both gushing over it to the point of feeding each other bites from our plates to share the greatness. As we walk out I pat my belly, feeling stuffed. "That was amazing."

"I'm glad you read about it, no one should miss out on that food," he says and smiles down at me.

"Keys, please," I state sweetly when we arrive at the car. A frown turns Colin's mouth down, making me giggle. "It's my turn. You had yours. Come on... hand 'em over." Reluctantly Colin retrieves the keys from his pocket and sets them in the palm of my hand as if they were made of gold.

"Be good to her," he whispers. I groan in mock annoyance at his show of testosterone before walking to the driver's side. When we're both buckled in I start the engine and carefully ease into first. One touch of the gas pedal and we surge forward. The power this car yields is like nothing I've ever experienced before. It grips curves with ease and seems to move forward on its own accord with little assistance from the gas pedal. Now I understand why Colin looked like he was having an orgasm the entire drive here. This piece of machinery is all power and seduction. It's a trip to drive. People check you out as you drive by them as if you just lost a hundred pounds and became a supermodel. I like it.

The entire drive--more like race--back, Colin's hand plays with the hair at the nape of my neck. "You look extra hot driving this car," he grins, checking me out.

"You didn't look so bad yourself."

"Before we return this we're taking a picture together in it," he declares excitedly as we enter Searsport.

PAST

2012
August

Tuesday morning I'm anxious when I wake up. I meet with the attorney today. I shower and dig through the haphazard selection of clothes I grabbed, searching for something classy to wear. Eventually I settle on a plain blue cotton summer dress and sandals. I sweep my hair up and away from my face into a loose French twist, put on some light makeup, and pace around the cottage for three hours until it's finally time to leave.

"So what you're telling me is that you want to fill out all the paperwork for divorce now but you don't want to file it?" Joe Jowett asks.

"Yes, that's correct. I want it all ready to go in case I need it." I nod.

"Elle, you're going to have to explain what exactly is going on." He arches an eyebrow at me. I sigh in dissatisfaction. I don't know if I can tell him everything, given I'm a missing woman.

"You can't share any details of our relationship can you? Even if I might happen to be a missing person?" I venture.

"Confidentiality clause says no, I can't share what we talk about," he nods.

"Well, I inherited a lot of money and assets over the last ten years. My husband had me committed seven months ago and I escaped because he granted himself Power of Attorney stating that I was a danger to myself, suicidal." My cheeks burn with humiliation but I continue. "This gave him access to all my funds that I've kept separate from him. I withdrew the cash that isn't tied up...but he could still sell the house and try and go after the investments I have, leaving him a very rich man. Unless he finds me, he can't access any of that. If he finds me and locks me up again under the pretense that I'm a lunatic he will clean me out because he can. So, I'd like all the necessary papers drawn up to protect myself and my assets so if he should come after me I can call you and put everything in motion. To save myself," I explain hesitantly.

"I see. I will need you to undergo a psychiatric evaluation to have on file stating that you are of sane mind, as a back-up to filing for divorce. As all the money and assets are in your name only. I see how Power of Attorney was his only legitimate option to gain access to it all. He needs you alive."

"Speaking of that, currently he doesn't. My will leaves most everything to him and my sister. My sister recently passed away. So now everything goes to him. I need a new will drawn up, too."

"Very well. Can you come back tomorrow for a psych evaluation and to do the will? I think we can take care of the divorce papers and asset protection today," he explains. He is very straightforward with me which I appreciate.

"Yes, I can be back tomorrow anytime," I breathe.

"How will you be paying?" He asks matter-of-factly.

"Cash." I state.

He smiles, nods his head and says, "Let's get started."

After a long afternoon of hunting down all my assets without calling my investment broker, we finally we have everything I need in place ready to go. Joe has set up the appointment for the evaluation for tomorrow morning so that there is record of me being mentally stable through this whole process. I'm not taking any chances. By the time I get home I'm emotionally exhausted and fall into bed without eating dinner or changing.

Wednesday at ten in the morning I head back the offices of Jowett and Cutler. The doctor Joe found on such short notice also happens to be a legend in the mental health world. Or so he tells me. They usher me into a conference room to wait for him.

"You must be Elle," he says and extends his hand to me. I take it, giving him a firm handshake.

"Yes and you must be Dr. Morgan."

He nods and sits in the chair next to me. "Mental Status Examination evaluates an individual's cognitive function and screens for cognitive loss. It will test your orientation, attention, calculation, recall, language, and motor skills. An individual can score a maximum of 30 points on the test; a score below 20 usually indicates cognitive impairment. Are you ready to begin?" he asks.

"Yes, please."

I was asked how I'm feeling, or how I'm eating and sleeping. If I worry a lot, have excessive--or not enough-- energy throughout the day. If I have a family history of mental illness and various other questions. I was honest and upfront about the suicide attempt, treatment for that, how I had grown and changed and how I'm dealing now.

Forty minutes later we're finished and twenty minutes after that he declares me a person of sane mind. Obviously. An hour after that, all the findings have been recorded and notarized and are put into a thick file with my name on it. I can't help but think that folder contains my real freedom should I need it: sanity, divorce, and all my assets.

"Joe, thank you so much. I feel better already," I tell him as he walks me to the elevators.

"You're very welcome, Elle, I'm sorry you've had to endure the things you have." He looks sincere. "Remember, you need to have a way to get in touch with me if something happens. I doubt if you're carted back to the hospital they will permit you to call your lawyer."

"Yes. I've thought of that too and I'm working on it. I'll let you know what to expect if the worst happens." He puts one arm around my shoulders, gives a quick squeeze, and then backs away as the elevator doors open.

"Bye." I chirp feeling better than I have in a long time. I feel in control and I like it.

"Bye, Elle."

The elevator doors cut us off and the elevator takes me down to the lobby. I again feel emotionally drained, but also like I've accomplished something important. I head back to my rental feeling like I've finally taken control of part of my life. I've finally taken charge and I will do whatever it takes to not feel hopeless again.

I celebrate my little victory that evening by indulging in a bottle of my favorite wine and cooking myself a delicious steak dinner. I bring it out to the deck and sit listening to the ocean while I eat in peaceful solitude. When I finished dinner, I dug through my suitcase and with my list in hand took it to the fridge and hung it there. Tomorrow I'll start.

PRESENT

ELLE

DAY 18

Before returning the car we'd stopped by Ben's place and he'd taken a picture of us in it together. Jenna had been over and had easily convinced me to let Ben take her for spin around the block before we left. When they returned, Ben and Colin had blabbered on eagerly about what a fine piece of engineering the car was. Jenna and I had roared with laughter watching the two of them act like teenagers.

This morning at the gym Jenna had shown up, declaring that she wanted to be badass like me. Colin spent the better part of our workout getting her up to speed and trying to get her to focus on what we were doing versus drooling over all the rock hard male bodies beating bags surrounding us.

"How do you do it?" she asks breathlessly from our hour of training.

"It gets easier." I snicker.

"Not the workout hussy, the men!" she chortles.

"I don't do them," I drawl.

"I mean, how do they not distract you. It's like hot man central in here."

"I'm kinda hooked on my own hot man." I grin at her and widen my eyes pointedly.

"Yeah, Colin is pretty amazing."

"Yeah, he is." I smile.

"What are you two up to today?"

"I believe today is 'get a tattoo' day." I chirp.

"What?!" she squawks in horror.

"I just have to get one. It doesn't have to be big," I reply. Truth be told I'm a little nervous. I don't have any tattoos and I imagine it's going to hurt like hell.

"What are you getting?" She asks wide eyed.

"I don't know yet." I shake my head. "I can't think of a single thing I want."

"Jesus, Elle. Do you really have to do everything on the list?"

"No, I don't have to... but I'm going to." I state.

"Ready, babe?" Colin asks and throws an arm over my shoulder.

"As I'll ever be," I shrug while plastering a nervous smile on my face.

"Eh, it won't be that bad." His attempt at comforting me is lost in the nerves attacking my body at the moment. I turn my attention back to Jenna.

"All right well, see you tomorrow, Jenna?"

"Do I have to?" she whines.

"Come on... we can be badass together!" I call over my shoulder.

"Fine. Tomorrow," she relents.

The Animated Canvas tattoo shop is buzzing, literally. Tattoo artists sit hunched over customers, needles piercing skin, creating artwork to last a lifetime. I flip a few more pages in the look book provided to me from Axe, the man who will tattoo me. I'm a little concerned that a man named Axe will be doing anything to me, quite frankly, but Colin assures me that he is the best at his trade.

"I don't see anything I want," I huff. The hazel of Colin's eyes temporarily soothes my frustration.

"Do you trust me?" he questions.

"You know I do."

"Then let me pick something out." He pleads.

"Umm, I'm not sure that's the most brilliant idea," I scoff. "This is permanent."

"Elle, I'll get the same thing if you let me do this," he returns. Now I'm intrigued.

"Well, what is it?"

"A surprise." He says.

"Wait, you want me to get a tattoo and not know what it is until it's on me!?" The shrill of my voice startles even me.

"Yup," he replies coolly. I stare at him for five heart-pounding seconds before my mouth betrays me.

"Okay." *Dear God, Jenny, what the hell have I just agreed to?* Colin doesn't hesitate, leaving me standing alone to speak with Axe privately. Heads nod and hands shake and then he calls me over and motions for me to lay on the table.

"Where would you like it?" he asks; his voice is rough.

"How big is it?" I mumble. He holds his hands up demonstrating about three inches to me.

"How bout here?" I lift my shirt and point to the left side of my rib cage. At least clothes will hide whatever it is I'm getting if I put it there. Axe nods and then gets to work with Colin making a stencil of sorts. Axe transfers it onto my skin and looks to Colin for approval.

"Perfect." With his response I'm laid back on the table,

Colin's hand strangled in my grip as I hear the needle start buzzing. When the needle hits my skin I clench his hand even harder and squeeze my eyes shut, scared that I'll flinch and make a mess of the tattoo. To my surprise, though, it doesn't really hurt. My eyes fluttered open as Colin's soft chuckles fill the air.

"Not so bad is it?" he asks and grins down at me, bearing that insanely sexy dimple.

"I guess not," I say, still keeping as still as possible. It feels like a mild sunburn being slapped, that stinging sensation it would leave behind. Colin entertains me with conversation for forty-five minutes until Axe declares I'm done.

"Wash with Dial twice a day for a month but other than that keep it as dry as possible. It will itch after a week or so, DO NOT SCRATCH IT," he instructs gruffly as he tapes a paper towel over it.

"Can't I see it now?" I beg.

"Not yet," Colin answers.

"Ready man?" Axe asks Colin.

"Yes." Colin goes through the same preparation that I did, taking care that I don't get a sneak peak. I sit in the chair next to the table he's on while Axe tattoos the inside of his bicep.

"Don't look, Elle," Colin chastises as I perk up and try to get a glimpse.

"Why so secretive, it's already on me." I huff at him.

"Just wait."

Another forty-five minutes later we are taped up, cash is exchanged, and we're heading out the door together with matching tattoos that I still haven't seen. I'm in agony waiting for this big reveal.

"Colin, this is ridiculous," I pout, walking back to the cottage.

"We're almost home, Elle, what's the difference now?"

"Irritating!" I sing, making him laugh.

I push the key into the lock and turn, blowing through the door full tilt towards the bedroom's full-length mirror. Colin stays close at my heel until I stop abruptly to pull my shirt off. Standing in front of the mirror, watching him smile the entire time, he pulls the tape from my skin and gently lifts the paper towel away.

"I'll never let you go" is scrawled three inches long down the side of my ribcage. The skin is still an angry red color, puffy and irritated-looking. My gaze drifts up to Colin's in the mirror. I suck in a sharp breath as I'm caught up in a tornado of emotion. He has the same thing on his arm. They are simple, black ink only, but the meaning of the words are anything but. Bending at the waist, his lips brush where my neck meets my shoulder. I pivot, turning to face him. "Perfect," I breathe just as his lips come crashing into mine.

PRESENT

ELLE

DAY 19

"I look like a hooker," I bristle as I exit Jenna's bathroom.

"How else are you going to get someone to say something lewd to you?" she says in a deadpan voice. I roll my eyes at her and tug on the bottom of the dress that barely hits my thighs.

"I think this outfit might be overkill." I whine.

"Shut up. You look fabulous. You're smokin'." She coos.

Teetering in my four-inch heels I round the corner to the living room. Ben and John whistle and cackle at me. Colin just looks mad. His jaw ticks and his lips are gathered into a thin line.

"Quit it. This was all Jenna's doing," I complain.

"You look hot," John gushes, making Colin turn another shade red.

"Yeah Elle, if you were a book cover you'd be a best seller!" Ben laughs.

"You're not leaving this apartment like that," Colin states through a clenched jaw.

"That's what I said!" I huff, throwing my arms up in frustration.

"Jenna," Colin booms.

"Yeah?" Her head pops around the corner.

"Fix this." He points at me.

"Get over yourself. She stays as is," she challenges.

Colin strides over to me looking less than thrilled. "What exactly is this supposed to accomplish again?" He waves his hand up and down my body.

"Someone deserving a drink thrown in their face?" I offer.

"I'll let you throw a drink in my face if you change." He challenges.

"That doesn't count, Colin, and you know it. Do I really look that bad?" I ask self-consciously looking down at myself.

"No, you look that good. That's the problem." He runs his hand down the open back of my barely-there dress, sending a shiver through me like a burst of electricity. I can't help but smile up at him. "Do you even have underwear on?"

"If I promise you can take me home and personally remove this dress for me to find out immediately after throwing a drink in someone's face will it make you feel better?" I propose. I think the dress is making me feel saucy and bold. His jaw's still set. I watch it tick again before he visibly relaxes and grins at me.

"Deal." He touches his lips to mine, teasing me, and pulls away before I've had enough.

"Let's go then." I grab his hand and tug. I want to get this over with so we can get back to kissing. The four of us file out of Jenna's apartment to The Underground.

It's loud, dark, and murky in the club. Like someone let

the fog machine blow for too long. Jenna and I have given the guys strict orders to stay on the opposite side of the club from us until drinks have been thrown. Colin is less than thrilled with this idea but surprisingly he does as told. Sitting at the bar with Jenna as we order our second round of drinks, I can feel his stare boring a hole through me. Turning slightly in my stool I catch his heated gaze. It's hot knowing he's watching me, that he wants to be at my side but can't. There's something about the thumping club music, a sea of undulating bodies on the dance floor, and knowing Colin and I can't do anything but admire each other that turns me on. It's strange being able to feel him all the way across the room. As I'm lost in his stare I notice his eyes narrow and his hands clench into fists at his sides. I snap my eyes from Colin to my left.

"Wanna dance?" a guy shouts over the blaring music. He's cute in a frat boy kind of way and looks to be somewhere in his twenties. Jenna nudges me off the stool towards him.

"Don't forget this!" she shouts, handing me my half-full martini and winking. I grab it from her hands just as the guy tugs me through the crowd causing my drink to slosh a bit. When he finds a spot near the middle he stops and faces me.

"You're hot." His eyes are glassy and unfocused and it scares me a little. His hands come to my waist gripping my hips tightly as he tries to move us to the music. He pulls my hips closer into his and starts grinding on me without restraint. I'm awkwardly holding one arm up to keep my drink from spilling and my torso is leaning away from his. His hand slips from my hip and works its way up my ribcage. With my free hand I swat it away. The lights are blinking and flashing and making me feel like I'm having a seizure and I can't find Colin. Maybe this was a terrible idea afterall.

His hand comes back, trailing up my ribcage inching towards the outside of my breast.

"Hey," I warn.

"Aww, you know you like it," he slurs.

"Let go." I've had enough. I'd rather someone just says something rude to me at the bar. I feel sick having someone else's hands on me. He doesn't let go though. His fingers dig into my hip and his mouth descends on my neck. It's vile and I force down the bile rising in my face. "I said stop!" I yell and, using my free hand, I push on his chest hard. "Stop!" I yell again. He stumbles back a step, eyes wild, and slams into Colin's chest. A wave of relief washes over me at Colin's presence. I lift my drink and splash its contents in the grabby guy's face. Gasps and squeals ring out around us and people clear away from us.

"Cock tease," the guy sneers, wiping the liquid off his face. All of Ryan's words come rushing back to me. I feel small and insignificant. I'm trembling in Jenna's ridiculous heels. It happens in slow motion almost in beat with the blaring music. Grabby guy lurches towards me and faster than I can fathom Colin steps between us and clocks the guy right in the face, sending him to the floor in a crumpled mess. He rips the glass from me and tosses it on the guy before bending and throwing me over his shoulder. He carries me with ease quickly out of the club. I'm still stunned when he sets me down outside.

"Elle, are you okay?" he questions, concerned. I snap out of my haze and look at him.

"Uh." I mumble.

"Something happened. You looked pissed, then you froze and looked terrified," he says, worried.

"Ryan," I breathe. "It was Ryan all over again." Colin pulls me close, snaking his arms around my middle and holds me tightly. I try to suck in deep breaths to calm my nerves.

"Let's get out of here," he whispers in my ear. I nod my head yes into his chest, inhaling his scent one last time before I let go. He gently tugs my hand to get me moving but I stop and remove my shoes first so I can walk without hurting myself.

"Did you cover my butt?"

"What?" he chokes out.

"When you carried me... did you cover me or did I just flash everyone in there?" I watch his ribs shake with laughter before he can speak.

"I covered your butt." He chuckles.

I blow out a sigh of relief and take Colin's hand in mine.

"Elle..." he trails off.

"Mmmhmm?"

"You can't freeze. If that had been Ryan, you can't freeze. You need to fight, like we've trained," he says. Concern laces his words.

"I know you're right but can we deal with that tomorrow? I don't want to ruin tonight anymore," I tell him honestly.

"Babe, tonight's not ruined. Plus, now that I know you're panty-free I'm taking full advantage when we get home." The devilish grin on his face lightens my mood instantly.

"Then let's get home." I wink.

PRESENT

DAY 20-21

"Get that," he groans and nudges me awake.

"What?" I yawn.

"Your phone. It keeps beeping," he mumbles into his pillow. I reach out to the nightstand and tag the phone. Flipping it open I press it to my ear. "'Lo?" Nothing. "They hung up," I mutter.

"It didn't ring, Elle. It beeped." I open my eyes, letting them adjust to the light and rub them vigorously. Jenna has been blowing up my phone texting me. I shoot her a quick message that I'll call, we're still sleeping, and I'll talk to her later. Almost instantly it beeps at me. Sighing, I pull the phone back open and read, "It's picnic day. Meet us at the beach at four."

Colin's arm swings over my waist and he drags me backwards into him, spooning me.

"What'd she want?" he murmurs in my ear. His hand drifts up and down from hip to ribs always lingering on my tattoo.

"Picnic day. Beach. Four," I breathe deep, enjoying his trailing fingers.

"What time is it?" His hand slips down between my thighs.

"Noon," I rasp as he kisses the back of my neck.

"Plenty of time then," he whispers before his fingers start working their magic.

My pulse quickens and I moan into his teeth as we kiss. He takes his time exploring my body ankle to mouth with his tongue, the electricity sparking off him sending currents through me. His defined muscles flexing as he moves, I can't tear my eyes away. Watching him is carnal. He pins my wrists above my head as he enters me, his eyes never leaving mine. It's intimate and leaves me dizzy and struggling for air. His slow movements tease me as he takes his time loving me. Slow and sweet and gentle. He dips his head to my ear and runs his tongue up my neck, circling my earlobe. "Come with me, Elle," he commands low and rough.

My hips buck wildly as his pace picks up and moments later we're exploding together. Colin collapses on top of me. I trail my fingers over the muscles of his back and kiss his neck lightly, trying memorize every divot and hollow of his frame.

"I love it when you do that," he sighs.

"What?"

"Run your hands over my skin like that." He says softly.

"I love it too," I murmur and shift. "It's almost one. We should get up. I have food to make."

"Danishes?" he asks hopefully.

"Hmm... I don't know.... will you help?" I wink.

"Anything for a Danish," he answers playfully.

I smack his behind, giggling. "Up then, we have work to do!"

We actually managed to make a batch of Danishes, a cheese, fruit, and cracker plate, and grab a bottle of wine before needing to meet Ben and Jenna at the beach. I was thoroughly impressed with us. Us. It's a funny word. A short one, but it carries so much meaning behind it. I snap out of my thoughts as I feel Colin's hand collect mine.

"Penny for your thoughts."

"Oh it was nothing, really."

"You're a terrible liar, Elle." He chastises.

I smirk at him. "I was thinking about the word 'us.'"

"What about it?"

"That it's a tiny word with a big meaning...and that when I think of me or you... it's as an 'us.' Now...where's my penny?" I ask playfully.

"I think that particular thought is worth a lot more than a penny," he says and kisses the top of my head as we hit the beach and look for Ben and Jenna.

"Hey! Over here!" Jenna's voice carries across the beach.

"Hi, guys. Good spot," I tell Jenna as we spread out another blanket.

"Ben found it." She beams.

The four of us make ourselves comfortable as Jenna and I unpack the feast we've packed. The spread we concocted is delicious and filling. By the time we're ready for the Danishes I'm not sure I have room for another bite of anything.

"Oh," Ben moans, mouth full of Danish. "These are heaven."

"Seriously, you guys made these?" Jenna asks in awe.

"Yup. We learned in that cooking class," Colin beams.

"Are there more?"

"There's two for everyone...because Elle's bad at sharing pastries." Colin laughs.

"Gimme." Ben swipes his second Danish from Colin's hand.

Ben, Jenna, Colin, and I hang out on the beach together enjoying the view and company until all three bottles of wine are empty.

"Well, we should head home," Jenna says and stands, brushing sand from her pants.

"Oh yeah, it's hot sex time!" Ben says and Jenna shoots him daggers as Colin and I burst out laughing.

"TMI!" I chuckle. I help Jenna load their stuff back into their bag and we say goodbye promising to train tomorrow together.

"It's so peaceful out here," Colin says and squeezes me into him.

"Mmmhmm."

"Elle, let's knock two things off the list." He murmurs close to my ear.

"Which ones?"

"Why don't we sleep out here tonight and watch the sunrise together?" He offers.

"I didn't pack anything for us to keep warm with though."

"I did." He says with an adorable glint in his eye.

"You did, seriously?"

"I thought it'd be romantic," he stammers. He looks as though he's second guessing himself.

"It is. I just... you're always one step ahead of me," I say and grin.

"Hang tight babe." Colin runs up to the car leaving me on the beach quietly enjoying the sound of the surf. When he returns he has a pillow and one sleeping bag.

"Ahh... where's the other one?" I question.

"It's a two-man sleeping bag," he says and winks.

"Those exist?" I squeak, twisting my face up.

"Yup, now climb in here with me." He spreads the sleeping bag on top of our beach blanket and strips down to his boxers before crawling into the bag. Watching him strip never gets old, my heart still pounds and my breath catches in my chest. He's stunning, but beyond that he's so much more. I don't know how I got so lucky but I'm running with it. He motions for me to join so I stand, pull my shirt off, and drop my pants.

"This is as naked as I get," I tease. Colin's heated expression makes me want to take that statement back immediately. I can feel the sexual tension as his eyes roam my body. I shimmy into the bag with him, resting my head on his shoulder. I struggle to control my breath. The feel of his skin on mine makes me feel bold and devious. "When the sun sets, the panties come off," he breathes in my ear. I run my hand down his torso and let it rest on his erection before lightly stroking him through his boxers. "Think you can make it till then?" I whisper. He cocks his head and his lips collide with mine. I can feel all the love and desire he holds for me in his kiss. He rolls us until he's on top of me. His mouth never leaves mine. I expose him through the hole in his boxers as he pushes my panties to the side and slips in. I've never made love on a beach before. The sound of the surf and the stunning sky combined with the salt air and risk of being seen heightens every sense as he languidly rolls his hips withdrawing and entering again and again. Tremors wrack my body as I cling to him until I can't hold back any longer and I let the pleasure blast through me. He finishes with a low animalistic growl that makes my belly whoosh. We lay spent and breathless, twisted together.

The first stars of the night sky become visible and as I stare up at them, completely satisfied and held tight in Colin's strong arms, a lonely fat tear rolls down my cheek. I'm overtaken with emotions. Safety, love, adoration, tenderness, and happiness.

"What's wrong?"

"Nothing..." I sniffle, "nothing's wrong... that's why I'm crying. Everything right now in this moment is right. It's amazing. I'm not sure I remember a time ever really feeling like this." He pulls me to his chest and twines our legs together but says nothing. There's nothing more to say. We stare at the stars together and watch the sky grow velvety and dark in each other's arms until his breathing is steady and even and I know he's fallen asleep. I roll onto my hip, slinging an arm and leg over him, put my ear to his heart and listen to his ever-present heartbeat until I finally drift off.

"Elle," Colin whispers gently.

"Mmm?"

"Wake up." He whispers again.

I open my eyes to the most heavenly sight. At the horizon the water sparkles deep orangey-pink before graduating shade by shade to a brilliant yellow. The sun's reflection on the water is impressive. It sits just above the water hovering in a cone of color before meeting the blue of the sky.

"Striking, isn't it," Colin comments.

"Yes." Seagulls call and waves rush the shore making a perfect soundtrack to the rising sun. We cuddle together in silence watching it rise for twenty minutes.

"I need to stretch," I yawn.

"Let's grab breakfast before we head home. I hear there are fresh made Danishes at the café." He winks.

"Perfect," I agree, leaning in to kiss his perfect lips.

Finally arriving at the cottage to change before hitting the gym, Colin's first action is crossing off three more things from the list. Watching him strikethrough the text gives me the most insane feeling of accomplishment.

PRESENT

DAY 22

"You really slept on the beach?"

"Yeah," I reply, my voice breathy.

"That's stupidly romantic," she sighs dreamily.

"Yeah."

"Girls! MOVE! Elle practice those right hooks. Jenna, light on your feet, dodge!" Colin booms at us. Jenna and I smirk at each other and resume sparring. We continue on for ten more minutes before Colin's patience for us flees the scene completely. He sends Jenna off with Ben to continue training and pulls me aside.

"Elle. I'm going to throw you in the ring with someone."

"Uh. Who?" I ask.

"A stranger. I want you to focus on what you've learned."

I'm a little leery of what Colin's suggesting.

"Why?"

"Just get in the ring," he commands. He's in trainer mode, not boyfriend mode, so I obey. A large man enters the ring. He's wide, fleshy, solid, and completely intimidating. On top of his stature he doesn't look like a nice person, his eyes are hard and currently trained on me.

"Start," Colin clips.

The man glances at Colin quickly before stalking towards me. I dart right and try to throw an uppercut but he dodges it easily. "Worthless," he grinds. I stop moving, unsure I heard him right. He takes the opportunity to jab my shoulder, sending me flying. When I'm stable on my feet again I swing again, barely clipping his torso. "Pathetic," he sneers. I blink rapidly, trying to understand what's happening. He throws a left hook that knocks me to the floor. "Can't you do anything right?" he snarls. I scramble back as he approaches me, trying to breathe. I hop to my feet and swing wildly, trying to make contact. "How stupid do you think I am girl?" Tears start building and my vision blurs. "Go on, take a swing, we both know you'll fail." I stand frozen and he raises his gloved fist and punches me in the ribs. The words spewing from his mouth send me careening back to a life I don't live anymore. Panic passes through me but then Colin's voice rings out, "Fight back." Panic transitions into rage. Not at this man in front of me but at Ryan and at myself for putting up with him. I lunge and land a jab to his kidney before shifting my weight and launching an uppercut that connects with his jaw sending him a step backwards. I continue the well-practiced combinations that I've been slaving over and connect with each attempt I make. Giant scary man bears the brunt of my rage but it's only moments before he begins to fight again. Two quick jabs to the face and I'm on my ass again panting, tears streaming down my face.

"Enough. Thanks, Chip," Colin shouts. I lift my head up, eyeing the big man. "Chip?" I question. How does a menacing man like that have a name like Chip? He nods at me and exits the ring, leaving me a heaving pile of emotions on the floor.

"You all right?" Colin's handsome face appears above mine.

"You're an asshole," I huff.

"You needed to know how to fight through it."

"Still an asshole," I clip.

"You're really mad, aren't you?" he pushes. I shove up and stalk past him to the locker room. "Elle!" he shouts after me but I don't bother stopping. I shower, change, and drag Jenna out the door without a word to Colin.

"What was that all about?" Jenna asks, wide-eyed.

"I don't want to talk about it."

"Okaaay. Well, what do you want to do then?"

"Read a book out loud," I answer curtly.

"List?" she asks hesitantly. I let out a sigh, trying to put a nicer tone to my voice. She didn't do anything wrong, I'm not upset with her.

"Yeah."

"Well, I know just the place for that! Let's see if the library will let you read at the kids' reading hour today." I look over to my friend and genuinely smile. She never pushes, and she always cheers me up.

"All right. Thanks, Jenna."

She links her arm through mine and leads the way.

The Searsport library is quaint. The old brick structure screams history. When you walk up the granite steps and open the door it's cozy and inviting. Jenna talks to the librarian briefly before coming back to me.

"All set. Reading hour is in thirty minutes so she suggested you look through the stack of books picked out and choose three to read."

"Thanks, Jenna."

"Hey, everyone fights and everyone makes up," she says pointedly. I nod my understanding as we make our way to the children's room. I used to think that by now I'd have at least one little one of my own but Ryan's behavior had quickly changed my mind about ever wanting to procreate with him. How could I justify bringing a child into a home full of hatefulness? It had hit me hard, realizing that I didn't want him to father my children, but as always I conceded to the fact and took the necessary precautions. Jenna takes a seat near the back while I thumb through the stack of books. Parents with their children begin to file in as I pick a third book and make myself comfortable. As the room fills in I watch as parents gush over their kids. Loving them is easy. I'd given anything to be a kid again. Life was simple and easy. The world was innocent and no matter how many times you failed at something as a child the ability to pick yourself back up and have another go comes naturally. I'd give anything to have that back. After a quick introduction the kids settle into silence and I begin to read. They make the cutest little noises, little ooo's and aahh's, and for forty minutes are completely entranced in the stories I read. It's calming reading out loud to children. They're so happy and involved in simply listening to your voice. When our time is up three of the children race up to me, grinning foolishly and give me big hugs.

My anger at Colin has dissipated remotely and I'm not fuming any longer.

"You have a great reading voice," Jenna compliments as we exit the library.

"I really enjoyed that actually. The kids were adorable."

"I'm going to miss you when you leave," she commiserates, changing the subject. I turn to face her.

"Maybe I won't leave then. I like it here."

"What about your job?" she questions.

"I can always try to find one here, right?"

"Would you?"

"I've given it some thought, yeah," I inform her. She squeals in delight and gives me a fierce hug.

"That would be awesome! I can't imagine going back to life before you," she gushes.

"I love you, Jenna."

By the time I arrive back at the cottage Colin is there waiting for me. Before I enter I watch him through the window pacing back and forth dragging a hand repeatedly through his hair then pinching the bridge of his nose.

"Hi."

"Elle. I'm sorry..." he immediately starts.

"Shh. I need to talk," I cut him off. "I understand what you were trying to do, I really do. I guess what you don't understand is what it was like living in the kind of relationship I was in with Ryan. I never knew what would set him off. I was never good enough. My days were mostly spent filled with fear of what might happen. When someone tells you they hate you repeatedly for years on end it... it changes you. I'm here because I didn't ever want to relive that and you threw it in my face and that hurts. You made me feel unsafe, Colin. I trusted you. Do you have any idea what it's like to live with someone like that? To sleep next to him night after night? To have to give myself to him?" My voice trembles as I finish. Colin looks terrified. I can tell he's been beating himself up over this all day and it makes me feel bad. I shouldn't care, I should worry about me, but I can't help it. The agony in his eyes is breaking my heart.

"Elle, I should have never put you through that. I'm so sorry. I didn't think it through. I was more worried about getting you to break through that wall of fear you hide behind than about what it might do to you." The anguish in his voice is almost unbearable to hear. "Please say you forgive me."

I wrap my arms around myself and watch his face twist in sorrow over his actions today. Ryan never had that look. Then again, I'm beginning to think Ryan never actually cared for me at all.

"I forgive you." The warmth and comfort his embrace brings as he rushes to me, holding me tight, is all I need to know that I really do forgive him.

PRESENT

ELLE

DAY 23

"Steal something? Really, Elle, this one does not sound like a fun one," Colin complains.

"You don't have to join me. Consider this the badass portion of the list."

"Elle, if you get caught..." His thought is lost to the wind blowing in from the sea.

"I won't," I state firmly, squeezing his hand.

"Why risk it?" he asks.

I sigh, knowing that it is a big risk given my situation.

"I'm going to do it, Colin." His jaw clenches in frustration at me and he stands from the couch, angry.

"Elle. Please." He doesn't finish his plea. He has a client in twenty minutes and needs to leave.

"Can we not fight?" I venture, standing up and placing a hand on his chest. His hazel eyes narrow on mine. "Call me if you need me," he grinds out through his teeth. I blow out a breath, nodding my head at him as he picks up his gym bag and heads to the door. He stops short, hand on the knob.

I move quickly to him, grab his attractive face between my hands and pull his head to mine. His kiss is hard and bitter but the more I mold myself to his lean frame the more his resolve melts, letting our lips move together in tenderness.

I walk down the street looking for a suitable place to steal something. It's not as easy as one might think. I feel like I already look guilty of something and I haven't even stepped foot in a shop yet. I take a deep breath to renew my resolve as the bell dings above the door to a cute card and stationery shop. I lazily walk around touching and looking at things.

"Can I help you find anything?" the clerk asks.

"Ah, no, just poking."

"Let me know if you need something," she says happily.

Guilt consumes me. My palms sweat and I go back and forth with myself a million times about whether or not to do it. I wander through the funny card section and find the most perfect card for Jenna. There are two ladies from the fifties on the front with a chat bubble that reads: "Let's go somewhere and judge people." I actually snickered out loud before picking it up and moving around the end caps, looking for something small to pocket.

There is a display of key chains at the far end of the store, furthest from the register. A black one with stud and an image of a muffin under it catches my eye. It would be cute for Colin. I pick it up--my heart instantly starts hammering in my chest--and slip it into my pocket. Walking up to the counter, I give the card for Jenna to the clerk to ring up. I swear she knows. She's judging me and waiting for the right moment to call me out on taking something.

"Three eighty-five."

"What?" I stammer.

"The total is three eighty-five."

"Right. Sorry!" I pull my wallet from my purse and give her four dollars. She hands me my change and tells me to have a nice day before I practically dart to the door. The fresh air mixed with my pumping adrenaline makes me feel lightheaded. Looking over my shoulder numerous times I collapse onto a bench a block away.

"'Lo?" Colin's deep vibrato answers.

"I did it."

"Okay?"

"I feel like a crack addict or something. I'm all shaky and I feel terrible," I say. His boisterous laugh vibrates my ear through the phone. "It's not funny. I'm freaking out here."

"Elle. Go home. I'll see you there in a bit."

"Colin," I whine.

"You're fine. Go home," he says more sternly.

"Fine." I flip the phone shut, suck in a shaky breath and walk home. I pace nervously around the living room until Colin shows up two hours later. I'm just waiting for the sales clerk or the police to hunt me down. My nerves are completely shot. When he pushes through the door I bolt straight to him, crashing into his firm chest.

"Jesus, Elle, what did you steal that has you this worked up?" he chuckles, wrapping his arms around me. I drop one hand and fish through my pocket for the key chain. Pulling it out, I hold it up for him to see. The laughter that follows is insulting to say the least. It takes Colin ten minutes to really catch his breath and calm down.

"A key chain? You've been a wreck for hours over a key chain?"

"It's not funny. I feel bad. Terrible, actually." My protest only makes him laugh harder.

"It's for you," I bark in irritation. His face sobers and his eyes crinkle with his smile.

"You think I'm a stud muffin, Babe?"

I pout and stomp my foot petulantly. The lopsided grin, sexy dimple, and twinkle in his eyes sets butterflies aloft in my belly. My ribs shake lightly before a belly laugh bubbles out of me.

"Yes. You're my stud muffin," I chortle, finally seeing the humor in my day. Colin's muscular arms wrap around my waist, pulling me down to the couch with him. "I'll be your anything," he murmurs before giving me a soul-searing kiss.

PRESENT

DAY 24

We signed our waivers, were weighed, and the length of the bungee cord was adjusted accordingly. We're strapped, briefed, assured, coached, coaxed, and sent to the platform. It feels like a death march. Then assured, coached, and coaxed again. The thrill of the adrenaline pumping through my veins is almost nonexistent compared to the sheer terror and stupidity of what I'm about to do. I'm going to die. I don't want to die! Why am I doing this? My hands are clammy and I'm trembling violently, part of my mind is screaming at me to turn back while I still can. This is certain death. I'm sure of it.

"FIVE, FOUR, THREE, TWO, ONE, BUNGEE!!" the man yells. I stall, rooted to the platform. "JUMP ELLE!" Colin shouts. At his encouragement I jump out as far as I can from the platform, scared shitless yet enjoying the free fall. The rush, the ecstasy, the adrenaline, the release. It's like having an orgasm and being in a car accident at the same time. I let out a blood-curdling scream as the bungee rope finally catches my ankles and I jerk, bouncing up and down momentarily until they haul me upright. Four minutes. That's the length of time from jumping until being on my feet again but I feel like an entirely different person. Triumphant and bold. Colin's proud grin mirrors exactly what I feel for accomplishing this.

I watch as Colin stands on the platform next. "FIVE, FOUR, THREE, TWO, ONE, BUNGEE!!" the man yells again. Colin doesn't hesitate. He leaps forward, plunging head first from the bridge. My heart lodges in my throat watching him. A million thoughts race through my mind, all having to do with losing him. He doesn't make a sound until his body forcibly jerks when the cord snags and even then it's just a loud grunt. I screamed like a little girl. His smile as he approaches me looks like it might split his face in half.

"That was amazing!" he gushes, high-fiving me.

"I know! It felt like I was being chased by zombies while having an orgasm!" I blurt, unable to accurately express what it felt like. "That's a surprisingly accurate assessment," Colin says and rolls with laughter at my description. He takes my hand and we head back to the car with shit-eating grins plastered to our faces.

The drive home was full of excited chatter over the thrill of free falling we experienced. I called Jenna and asked if they wanted to meet us out for dinner or drinks because we were still too amped up to go home.

"Oh my god, Elle! Look at your face! You look terrified," John snickers. Colin has showed the video he took of my jump to anyone sitting remotely near us at the Pig Pit.

"I was terrified," I clarify.

"I still can't believe you did it," Jenna snorts.

"You might want to close your mouth before someone takes it as an invitation," I laugh.

"You and Ben should give it a go. It's awesome," Colin interjects. Jenna shakes her head violently at the idea while Ben fist bumps Colin with excitement and I can't help but laugh. The bartender sets our drinks in front of the five of us.

"If tomorrow is something fun, I want in," Ben demands.

"Tomorrow I learn to shoot a gun."

"GUNS?! I'm in! When and where?"

"We're hitting the Thornville shooting range after my last client. 'Round three," Colin answers. John, Ben, and Colin continue discussing guns and ammo while Jenna and I catch up on key chains, cards, and workouts. Colin's hand stays draped over the back of my chair or on my thigh as always and I can't help but grin like a fool at how lucky I feel.

PRESENT

DAY 25

The leaves are just beginning to change colors. Lush greens now accompanied by various tints of oranges, yellows, and reds make our drive to Thornville pretty as scenery rushes past the car windows. Ben, John, and Jenna follow behind Colin and me.

Colin pulls into the parking lot of the barracks store, kills the engine, and jogs around to my side of the car to get my door for me. The five of us enter the nondescript store heading straight for the gun case.

"What can I do for you?" the clerk asks Colin.

"We need a pistol for her," he says and nods at me. The clerk rifles through the case before pulling out a pistol and setting it on the counter.

"This is a Glock 19. The pistol weighs twenty-nine ounces when it's fully loaded. It is capable for holding nineteen rounds and is a semi-automatic powerhouse. Basically small and light for your girl here."

"Pick it up, Elle. See how it feels." I take the gun from

the counter. It's heavy in my hand but I don't know what else I'm supposed to be checking for.

"Seems fine," I say. Twenty minutes later I'm the owner of a gun. The only snag had been filling out the paperwork but Colin has quietly advised me to just use his address as my permanent residence. Jenna had seen a handgun with a pink handgrip and decided she had to have it. Ben told her that's no way to pick a gun but she had no interest in listening and bought it anyways. To my surprise each of the guys owned at least one gun. I had no idea that Colin had guns but he explained that his dad and he used to go to the shooting range a lot growing up and he's very careful with them, keeping them locked in a gun safe at his place.

The Thornville range is in the basement of an unremarkable office building. Behind a metal door with its logo, the buzzing of fluorescent light is the soundtrack that accompanies our trek downstairs. The walls are pale yellow now faded and sickly looking. Already, I can hear very muffled gunshots. I listen with mild apprehension. It is a distinctive noise, not exactly a bang. It rebounds, echoing off the walls.

I plait my hair into a loose braid and secure it as Colin finishes setting everything up.

"Put your feet shoulder-width apart. Slight bend at the knees, and a small lean forward at the waist." Colin adjusts my stance for me. "Good. Keep your index finger off the trigger until ready to fire. Try to relax. Take a few deep breaths. When you're ready, squeeze the trigger on your exhale."

Colin steps away and I take three deep breaths while aiming at the paper target. I squeeze the trigger at the end of my third breath. The reverberation startles me and the recoil was tough to control, though I'd expected it. I hit the left edge of the target but only barely. Shooting again and again, I sniff the powder and strain to get a better shot. Sometimes I do pretty good; others, I'm way outside of the target. I keep tensing up right before the explosion. Colin is patient and gives me space to just practice when I shoo him away. He gently corrects my hold and position as necessary, resulting in me hitting the target more often. Once I get used to the feeling of it, I like the little rush I get each time I pull the trigger. It makes me feel competent and commanding.

Colin and John are both excellent marksmen. Their paper targets come back with perfectly clustered little holes in all the appropriate areas. Ben didn't even manage to fire his gun once. Jenna monopolized his time and couldn't quite get the hang of the whole thing. His patience with her surprised us all, I think.

"So how did you do?" Jenna asks as we file out.

"Not too bad. I hit the target, mostly, but some shots were just hitting the paper edge. I liked it though. I thought it was going to be scarier."

"I suck, but I had fun."

"We should keep coming, without the guys, and get really good and then blow their minds," I chuckle at her.

"Hey, I'm game if you are."

"Deal."

Colin's hand comes to the small of my back as we exit the building. The heat from his touch never fails to do funny things to my belly.

"You did good today."

"Thanks. I had a good time."

"Would you come again?" he asks.

"Definitely!"

"Are we still on for dinner at Blitz?" Ben hollers across the parking lot.

"Yeah! See you in a few!" I answer as we all pile into our cars to make the journey back home. Being out with my small but wonderful group of friends makes my chest swell. I can't imagine life without them anymore. It's such a simple thing, having a few good people to count on, but it makes such a difference in one's life. *I know it's been a while, Jenny, but I hope you're up there smiling down on me.*

PRESENT

ELLE

DAY 26

After tying our aprons on, we wet our hands and the clay and following instruction use our full strength, resting our hands against our thighs to provide stability while trying to center our lumps.

"You will know the clay is centered when you can wrap your hands around it and it spins smoothly," the teacher explains.

My opening is lopsided, and I have to close it up, re-center, and try again. Once I get a hole I use both of my hands to widen it. The clay is slick and smooth under my hands. Using gentle pressure as instructed I mold the clay into a wide bowl. It's very much a tactile experience. My fingers see by feeling the clay: its texture, pliability, responsiveness to pressure, shape, and moisture. Using a pottery wheel is a sensual, messy, satisfying experience.

I watch as Colin gets sprayed by the fine mist blowing off the wheel as he spins his lump of clay around trying to form something. His brow is furrowed as he focuses on what he's doing and his bottom lip is caught between his teeth.

"This isn't anything like Ghost," he whines when he catches me staring at him. A few other classmates join me in a fit of laughter at Colin's statement. The teacher moves behind him and guides his hands until his lump vaguely resembles a vase.

"When the piece is shaped to your satisfaction, slide a wire under the base and set it aside to harden up," she says.

Having pretty much given up hope of creating something stunning, Colin slides the wire under his to set it aside. As I finish mine to the best of my limited ability he leans in, brushing a kiss on my neck. "Looks good," he says low in my ear.

"Thanks." I slide a wire under my bowl and move it to the shelf to let it harden. At the end of our class the teacher lets us know that in two days we can pick up our fired and finished pieces.

After a delicious round of chili for dinner, Colin and I spend the rest of the evening snuggled into one another on the couch watching movies and quietly conversing about life and love, because when you stop and look around this life is pretty amazing. When we finally crawl into bed he takes mine hand in his and rests them over my heart.

"Feel that?" he whispers in the dark.

"Yes."

"That's called purpose. We're here for a reason." He kisses me once with tenderness before letting go of my hand and pulling my back tightly to his front. My chest swells with emotion at his words. My brain whirls one thought round and round like a tornado: I'm in love with this man. It scares me to realize how much he's become mine when I'm not sure how much time I have, knowing that I don't belong here. I push all my demons down and try to let myself enjoy the feeling of safety and love for the time being.

PRESENT

COLIN

DAY 27

Elle, Jenna, Ben, and I are headed now to Target. We're supposed to get kicked out of a Wal-Mart per Elle's list but Target is closer and we all agreed it was basically the same idea. We don't have a solid plan on how to do this but we're all pretty excited and convinced it will end up being a great story. Elle's chili was nothing short of amazing, however, chili comes with a written guarantee from me that if I eat it, the next day my ass will fall off and this morning I wasn't able to make it happen.

When we enter the store Elle grabs a cart and starts pushing it up and down aisles. We're flying by the seat of our pants here. I'm not sure what will come in handy so we're all just chucking things into the car. We're furthest from the restrooms when the pain hits me. No, no, no. This can't be happening.

"Elle." I groan. "Uh...I gotta go ." This pain feels different from my normal poop cramps. The peppers in the chili seem to be staging a revolt. My stomach knots in pain making me clutch my gut and double over.

"Are you all right?" Elle asks, concerned.

This is every man's worst nightmare. In some sadistic dash for freedom the peppers rip their way through my intestines, and before I can take a single step Elle's chili fires a warning shot and I freeze in horror.

"Holy shit, Colin!" Elle pinches her nose and her face turns red.

"Dude," Ben scolds as Jenna just makes an awful retching sound.

We're in the beer aisle, suddenly trapped in a noxious cloud the likes of which has never before been smelled. I'm afraid to move for fear that more of this vile odor might escape me. I shrug my apology to the three horrified people staring me down. "What?" I ask and resume walking to the main one, just as a woman turns down ours.

I don't know why, but I stop to see what her reaction will be to the nasty vapor that refuses to lift. I stand frozen again and watch as she walks into an invisible wall of odor so rancid that all she can do before coming to her senses is stand there blinking in horror. Without warning Elle, Jenna, Ben, and I begin to laugh. Big mistake.

It's hard to keep things clenched while laughing. With each burst of laughter an explosive fart bursts out of me. Suddenly things are no longer funny. "No!" I scream. "It's coming!"

Ben's laughter roars as I race towards the bathrooms, praying that I make it before the grand assplosion takes place. I'm prepared to do whatever it takes, push women and children out of my way to ensure I don't publicly crap my pants. I make it just in time and begin the floating above the toilet seat because my ass is burning so bad.

Thanking God no one came in while I was going, I exit the restroom, determined to somehow make Elle not think I'm the most disgusting human on earth when a store employee approaches me.

"Sir, you might want to step outside for a few minutes. It appears someone set off a stink bomb in the store." I can feel my eyes bug out but with everyone waiting just steps away rolling with laughter, I can't help but join them, causing a follow-up fart to escape. The employee takes one sniff, jumps back, pulling his shirt up to cover his nose and points at me accusingly and backing up a step.

"IT'S YOU!" he shouts, running off.

"Colin," Elle wheezes, trying to catch her breath. "Oh my god. I'm going to die of laughter." Her eyes are watering and mascara streams down her face.

"Holy shit dude. This is seriously the best day of my life!" Ben squeals as the employee returns with the manager in tow.

"Sir. We're going to have to ask you to leave the store," the manager states while trying not to gag.

"What?" I can tell my expression is nothing short of horrified.

"And please, don't come back." He waits as I glance over to everyone and then points to the door. "Out. Now."

Elle, Ben, and Jenna follow a good distance behind me as we exit the store, probably in fear that my bowels will kill them if set off again. I am utterly horrified that my ass just got us kicked out of Target. I can feel my cheeks redden with every step I take.

"You were right," Elle quips, trying not to laugh.

"Yup, funniest, most amazing, best story ever out of this!" Jenna bellows before doubling over in another fit of laughter. I slap my face and drag my palm down it.

"I am never eating your chili again," I say and shoot Elle a pointed look. The three of them stand there choking on their laughter and clutching each other for stability at my expense.

"I'm ready to go home," I say in a deadpan voice.

It took a bottle of Pepto Bismol and a lot of coaxing that I didn't think he was disgusting before Colin calmed down enough to enjoy the rest of our day after the Target incident.

It had taken me by surprise when Colin brought up the fact that my month was almost up. He held me close and asked me hesitantly what I was doing after the rental was up. I've thought it over a lot and talked to Jenna about it. I want to stay. When I told Colin that I plan on staying he was overjoyed, going on about how relieved he was to hear me say that.

I explained that I needed to find an apartment and a job and I might stay with Jenna until I could find something suitable. His face had dropped slightly, surprising me. Sure we spend our days mostly together, but he couldn't think that we'd just move in together after a month. He offered his place up until I found a place and I told him I'd think about it but I knew that I didn't want to rush things more than they already were.

As he held me firmly in bed that night my brain went into overdrive thinking about my life. I'll never go back to Ryan, but there are so many things to fix before I can really settle into my life here. I can't imagine a world without Colin, Jenna, and the guys, but they don't know the extent of what I'm up against either. His warm body pressed up against me, warming me. The air all but crackled every time we were near each other. How could I possibly tell him the rest without him thinking I'm insane, without him looking at me differently? Just before falling asleep his fingers had grazed the inside of my wrist and slid up through the palm of my hand until they pushed in between mine and interlaced together while he softly rubbed his thumb back and forth over the knuckle of my thumb. The intimate gesture sucked all the air from my lungs. I couldn't bear to lose him, to have this change in any way.

PRESENT

ELLE

DAY 28

My eyes fluttered open as warm soft kisses started at my shoulder blades moving down my spine before ending at the small of my back where the blanket draped across my hips. He made his way back up, following the same path before rolling me to him. His tongue softly pushed past my lips as his knee moved between my legs, pushing my legs apart. He settled himself there and paused. His kiss lights me on fire, and I can't stop from breathing my moan into his mouth.

"Morning, Babe." His voice is thick with sleep as he pushes inside of me slowly.

"Morning," I breathe. Feeling every solid inch of him inside me makes me pulse around him with the need for more. His lips descend on my neck, just behind my ear and a low guttural cry escapes me as he eases in and out. "So wet," he rasps. "Always ready."

Wrapping my legs around his hips and pulling him deeper into me as he rolls his hips is too much and not enough at the same time. I can't seem to ever get him close enough. "More," I pant. Colin slips an arm under me, pulling me closer to him and picks up his pace. It's wild and unrestrained and I find myself clutching him firmly to keep the rhythm. I can feel the telltale blush spread across my chest just before I come apart around him. I've never felt anything more intense in my life. When his body jerked with the force of his orgasm he collapsed against me panting heavily. His hazel eyes stare into mine, drinking me in like he's memorizing every inch of me as he brushes my bangs out of my face. "I love that."

"What?" I ask.

"You absentmindedly lick your lips when I check you out," he smirks. "It's hot." He dips his head to mine again, brushing a light kiss across my lips before rolling off to the side.

"We should shower."

"We?" he questions, raising his brow at me curiously.

"If you're up for it."

"Go!" he yells and hops out of bed, racing to the shower, leaving me in stitches at his enthusiasm.

Four hours and an intense sparring session at the gym later Colin, Ben, Jenna, and I are enjoying the weather, some music, and drinks on the patio at my cottage.

"Geez, Jenna, I had no idea. I have a really good lawyer if you want to meet with him."

"Well, he didn't really start stalking me until he noticed Ben around," she admits. Ben's hands are clenched in fists as his sides and his jaw ticks as Jenna speaks.

"I don't care about the whole slashing a tire bit, but I don't think it should be his," he grinds out.

"Oh stop. He won't do anything to me and you know it. He's just creepy."

"I agree with Ben. Why don't you just let us handle this creepy ex-boyfriend?" Colin asks.

"Because this will be so much more fun! Right Elle?!"

"Right," I say flatly. I am all for the slash-a-tire activity happening, but I'm not sure I think Jenna's stalker should be our target. Sure, he's deserving and all, but will he retaliate against her if he finds out, is what worries me.

"We won't go until dark."

Jenna and I take off in Ben's car around nine and head over to the location of her ex-boyfriend's truck. Colin, although irritated that we couldn't just pick a stranger and keep the danger level to a minimum, gave us the hunting knife he keeps in his trunk. Jenna parks the car a block away from the truck to keep from getting caught.

"Okay, so I just stab it right?" I ask as we're crouched behind the truck together.

"I don't know! I'm no expert here," she whispers back.

Sighing, I pull the knife from my coat pocket and unsheathe it. "It's not going to explode, right?"

"Elle...I have no idea. Just do it."

"I'm scared! You do it!" I hiss.

"It's your list, I just provided the tire for you. Now hurry up, I have to pee!"

I raise the knife and jab the tire with it. The force of my blow does nothing but bounce the knife back at me. Apparently tire rubber is extremely durable and takes a lot of force to penetrate. With Jenna chuckling quietly at me I try again, stabbing the tire with as much force as I can muster. There's a big hiss and a gust of wind, and then it's over. No pop, no explosion, not much danger and nothing melodramatic as the car sinks a few inches. Jenna and I look at each other as if we didn't do it right momentarily before I shrug. "I guess that's it." We scurry down the street to the car giggling about how lame slashing a tire is and spend the car ride home laughing over the huge letdown it turned out to be.

"There really wasn't much excitement was there?" Jenna snickers.

"I think crouching behind his truck was more exciting than the tire deflating," I laugh.

"Stupid jerk deserves a flat."

"Well then, mission accomplished," I snort.

The guys greet us at the door when we arrive back at the cottage. None of them look particularly happy but relief is etched in their faces when we come through the door. "So?" Ben asks, tapping one foot nervously.

"We did it."

"And..." he goads.

"It was kind of a letdown," I pout. "Nothing exciting happens when you slash a tire." I sigh in disappointment. Ben and Colin stare at us a moment before bursting into laughter at Jenna and I.

"What did you think was going to happen?" Colin asks.

"I don't know.... but something! It just hissed and deflated," I say and shrug.

"I'm a little sad this list is done. We have some good stories from it," Colin says and shakes his head sadly.

"Like your assplosion?" Ben chimes in.

"We agreed never to talk about that again," Colin spits, pulling me into a hug. "Sorry it wasn't as badass as you wanted it to be," he murmurs in my ear.

"Eh... it's all right. What do we have for dessert? I'm kinda hungry." Everyone laughs at my obvious need for sugar before joining me in the kitchen.

PRESENT

ELLE

DAY 29

"Pivot! Pivot Elle!" Colin shouts as I continue my combinations on the heavy bag.

We've hit the speed bags, double end bags, and tackled the more physical stuff too like push-ups and sit-ups already. My energy is waning fast and all I want to do is tell him to screw himself so I can stop.

"Break," he clips. "Rope...ten minutes."

I drop my arms and curse at him under my breath before picking up the jump rope and starting. By the time Colin thinks it's acceptable for me to be done I'm dripping with sweat, feel like throwing up, and unsteady on my legs.

"Good job today, Babe," he says, leaning in to kiss me.

"Yeah, no special treatment here," I complain, making him chuckle.

"What time will you be home?"

"Um," I say, still trying to catch my breath. "I have two appointments back-to-back to see apartments but I think I should be back around four or five."

"All right, I'll cook dinner so don't pick anything up," he instructs.

"Oh really?"

"I have a little surprise for you. I should be home by five thirty." He winks and turns away, leaving me at the entrance to the locker room. By the time I'm ready to leave I'm still grinning like an idiot. I love surprises and I can't wait for Colin's.

The realtor I met with was pleasant enough but the apartments she showed me were not at all what I was looking for. I had made it clear that I wanted something with an ocean view so that I could still open windows and hear and smell the ocean. Both apartments were further in town with an ocean view from the roof, maybe. They were smaller than the rental cottage too, which isn't a total deal breaker but if I'm setting down roots I want a guest room at the very least. By the end of the second showing I sensed the realtor was frustrated with me. Her heels clack obnoxiously down the stairs and her cheap suit reminds me of something Ryan's mother would wear. "It's all right to take our time and find something," I say calmly. "I'm not in a hurry, really, so why don't you get back to me this week with some more options?"

"Of course, Ms. Darling," she says and we part ways outside the second apartment with no love lost.

It's three thirty, Colin won't be home for another two hours, but I'm glad. It gives me time to get home, clean up a bit and change for him. I have no idea what he has up his sleeve but I want to look good for it. I can't help but smile as I walk back to the cottage.

I swing the door open, walk to the kitchen, and put my purse down. The list on the fridge is full of things that have been crossed out. All but one. The last one. It's not something I can do in a day but it's definitely happening. I feel it more and more each day. I breathe a sigh of relief and accomplishment at everything I've managed to do.

"You're a tricky little girl, aren't you? I've been looking for you. You're smarter than you look, using someone else's address," comes a deep voice that startles me. I turn on my heel and come face to face with a short stocky man with slicked back hair. "It's time to go home, Elle," he spits. Terror rips through me as he eases another step toward me.

"Who are you?" I demand. The gun. I have to get the gun.

"A friend of your husband's."

"Mick," I breathe, trembling.

"Ah, so you've heard of me then. Good, then you know better than to try anything stupid."

"Excuse me?" I take a step back and reach for the drawer behind me where Colin told me to keep the pistol loaded. If I can keep him talking maybe I have time to get it. He lunges forward snagging my wrist, gripping it harshly in front of him. My legs shake and my stomach churns as his grip tightens.

"I wouldn't do that unless you want to end up like your sister," he sneers. Everything snaps into place: Jenny's accident, my inheritance, being committed. His free hand pulls out a gun just as I cock my hand back to punch him. My fist connects solidly with his nose. A bone-crunching sound accompanies his grunt as I twist out of his hold and start to run. My heart beats erratically at the thought of him catching me. I'm two steps from the door when the hard metal grip of a gun comes down, landing at the base of my skull. Pain radiates through my body in waves and my vision starts to blur. All my thoughts zero in on Colin and how this will break him as my eyes roll back into my head and the world fades to black. I free fall to the floor in a heap.

Continued in Book Two: *Committed*, out now!

ABOUT THE AUTHOR

I am an avid reader, coffee drinker, and chocolate eater who loves writing. I received my B.A. from Simmons College-a while ago. I currently live in Maine, The Way Life Should Be!

I'm working on my sixth novel currently. I've published Saving Caroline, 30 Days, Committed, Tug of War and Dating Delaney.

I have a weird addiction to goat cheese and chocolate martinis, not together though.

I adore my dog. He is the most awesome snuggledoo in the history of dogs. Seriously.

I hate dirty dishes.

I like sarcasm and funny people.

I should probably be running right now... because of the goat cheese....and stuff.

I love hearing from you so please feel free to contact me!

www.klarsenauthor.com
@klarsen_author

https://www.facebook.com/K.LarsenAuthor